THE WINGED WARRIOR

P. A. Bechko

CHIVERS LARGE PRINT
Bath

CURLEY LARGE PRINT
Hampton, New Hampshire

Library of Congress Cataloging-in-Publication Data

Bechko, P. A.
  The winged warrior / P. A. Bechko.
    p. cm.
  ISBN 0–7927–1940–9 (hardcover)
  ISBN 0–7927–1939–5 (softcover)
  1. Flying-machines—Fiction. 2. Large type books. I. Title.
[PS3552.E24W56 1994]
813'.54—dc20   93–40606
                                                            CIP

British Library Cataloguing in Publication Data available

This Large Print edition is published by Chivers Press, England, and by Curley Large Print, an imprint of Chivers North America, 1994.

Published by arrangement with the Golden West Literary Agency in association with Laurence Pollinger Ltd.

U.K. Hardcover ISBN 0 7451 2203 5
U.K. Softcover   ISBN 0 7451 2214 0
U.S. Hardcover ISBN 0 7927 1940 9
U.S. Softcover   ISBN 0 7927 1939 5

Printed in Great Britain

To the Circle Z Ranch

THE WINGED WARRIOR

CHAPTER ONE

The day dawned bright and clear with a vibrant orange glow that rolled across the valley as if it had been blessed by the gods themselves. Monument valley at dawn. The huge monoliths rising from the valley floor like monsters frozen at the dawn of time. The light of the new day flowing over them from the east, casting heavy black shadows that lay across the land like threatening thunderheads though not even a tiny bit of a cottony cloud intruded on the broad unbroken expanse of blue overhead.

Omaha Jones took a deep breath where he stood on the precipice, arms securely strapped in place with stout leather thongs. Dressed ceremoniously for the occasion in elaborately beaded loincloth and leather leggings, he felt his lungs and chest expand with the sudden rush of incoming air. One last time he glanced sideways toward the lad who had climbed El Capitan with him, a young, strapping boy of only twelve summers. The wind was blowing steadily in Omaha's face in almost an omen of good fortune. The gods were smiling upon his venture, leading him to live his name, Omaha, against the wind.

Leaning forward, Omaha calmly, without

1

fear, stepped off the peak of El Capitan, leaving the young brave to stare after him in awe. For an instant Omaha dropped like a stone, the floor of the reddened valley rushing up to meet him with appalling speed. Then, suddenly, a gust of wind slipped beneath his wings and swept him heavenward even faster than he had dropped. The tautly stretched parchment-thin leather was holding. Not a single tear opened beneath the pressure of the wind and the pulling force of his weight as he was swept along on a north, northeasterly course. The sturdy framework, light but tough, splayed out over him and to either side above outstretched arms in a large, swept-back canopy that so closely resembled the V shape of a hawk's outstretched wings that it was patterned after.

Elated, Omaha stared down at the earth far below with fascination. He had known it was possible, as those who had tried it before him in far-off lands had known the same thing though they had not been able to prove it as he had. It was early spring of 1888 and he, Omaha Jones, had proved it could be done. Proved that flying was not just for the birds. Giving a wild, savage cry of victory, that hung on the wind that carried him along, he gloried in the feeling that birds had known for eons past. Omaha was soaring in body as well as spirit.

Minutes passed like seconds, and Omaha, now more secure with his position in the sky far above the valley, decided to see how much control he had over his path. He had expected to launch himself from the top of the towering peak of El Capitan and slide slowly back to earth. Never in his wildest hopes had he expected this. Already he had covered miles. El Capitan had become a peak in the distance among many. The boy left far behind would undoubtedly be wondering what would happen next, as Omaha himself wondered much the same thing.

Arms outstretched and swept at a slight angle back from his body, were useless. He had only the weight of his body to try and maneuver with. Never had he thought of the need to be able to control his single, overhead wing that would let him command the skies as the mighty eagle did. He had simply believed that that would come with the act of flying. The hawk did not seem to put effort in the direction of his flight as he glided effortlessly across the desert sky, often not flapping his wings for many miles. Omaha was confident that he too would master the art, it would just take a little time.

Feeling free, Omaha relaxed as a new gust of superheated air rose from the valley's floor, swinging him even higher into the morning sky. The sun blazed now in a fiery orb hanging low in the eastern sky as its heat warmed the waiting land. He felt the warmth creep into his outstretched limbs and craned his neck to see more of the earth below him as the wind carried him swiftly along and he remembered the work, and the arduous climb. It had been all worth it for just this moment.

The boy, Little Thunder, had climbed El Capitan with him. Together they had spent the entire day from before dawn until after dusk, fighting the reluctant mountain. First they would climb, then they would pull the precious wings carefully up behind their ascent. From the beginning, when the others in the tribe he had returned to from school back East had heard what he was determined to attempt to do, they had turned from him, declaring it as a useless undertaking. Little Thunder, though, had been interested in spite of the talk, and had taken advantage of every opportunity to be near Omaha, to watch the progress of the swept-back wings with fascination. Being a practical man and knowing he would at some time need assistance, Omaha had not discouraged the boy's interest.

Then, with the preparations finished, Omaha decided on his launching site. There could be no other than El Capitan. It was a long hard climb, but he had made it to the top once before, years earlier, when he had been not much more than a boy. His father, a white trapper, had wandered into the valley with his Indian wife and son. The tribe had been camped in the timber country to the northwest as it now was. Even then Omaha had wished to be able to touch the sky and had undertaken the climb with enthusiastic urgings from his father, and calm acceptance from his mother.

This time, though, the climb had been with purpose. Resolute, Omaha Jones and Little Thunder had mounted El Capitan, reaching the towering height as the sun was lost to view, leaving behind only the fading purples and pinks of what had been a spectacular sunset. In the dim grayness before the dark, Omaha and Little Thunder had quickly, but carefully, pulled the wings up behind them on the long cords that were attached to them and tied about their waists. Then the wings were tied securely to a huge rock to secure them against the night winds and they had settled down for the night.

Little Thunder had slept, but Omaha had lit a small fire on the exposed peak and prayed to every god he could think of. Never one to leave any avenue unexplored, he had prayed first to the Indian gods he had grown up knowing so well, then to the white man's God and the teachings of his father's people. Omaha Jones was half Sioux and half white, a fact he had decided long ago should double his expectations instead of limiting them. A half-breed was what he was, and he had heard about it often enough, but he was practical in matters of life. He sprang from both worlds, and logically that meant the gods of each should have an eye on him. Perhaps that would help him to succeed where others had failed before him. He had sung the chants of the Sioux before the fire, arms outstretched to the moonlit sky. He had knelt quietly on the stone peak as the moon had set, leaving only the stars to wink in the heavens above him, and prayed quietly to the God of the white half of him. He had prayed for victory, success, to soar among the birds, or, philosophically, at least a quick, honorable death should his step out into space end only in a crash to the rocky ground below. To end a cripple, unable to do anything else save work with the women of the tribe after such a glorious undertaking would be a crushing blow, worse than the failure itself. Finally, Omaha had stretched out upon the hard cold stone surface and, for a few hours, slept.

Even before the first faint streaks of dawn had touched the sky, Omaha had been up, preparing, and Little Thunder had been by his side, eager to do his smallest bidding. Carefully, Omaha had checked the wings one last time for any loose bindings or small holes in the surface of the tautly pulled

6

leather covering. Then, as a dim lighting had begun in the eastern sky, Omaha had lifted his wings to the edge of the peak and stepped inside the sturdy framework, hoisting it into position for Little Thunder to lash him in. In the stirring of the morning air the wings had been unwieldy, but with legs braced, knees locked, and a determined set on his face, Omaha had held his ground, reveling in even higher hopes of flight as the wind tugged at the partially attached wings, threatening to snatch him right off the peak of El Capitan and into the brightening sky. Little Thunder had worked quickly as he had taught him, lashing his arms securely to the wings as he stood within the squared wooden frame he had designed to protect his chest, should he be swept into something while in flight. The wings, rigid to allow him to glide but not flap, spread above him like a giant sun canopy coming to a rounded point above and before his head. The wing on either side of him swept back in a graceful curve, hawklike, and his legs would dangle free to allow for a birdlike landing. Had he used the design he had first come up with he would have been forced to lie within the framework and crash-land on his belly, which from a practical viewpoint had not been very appealing.

Standing on the edge of El Capitan's peak in beaded ceremonial breechclout and leggings he had had to trade for because he as yet had no woman to do such work for him, Omaha had watched the brightening of the eastern sky and quite unafraid stepped out into the abyss. The thrill of that instant had shot cold waves rippling throughout his body as he had momentarily plummeted earthward, then was snatched high into the air as the wind rose almost by the command of some supernatural force.

Now Omaha Jones rode the air currents with the ease of an eagle on outstretched wings. Far below the canyons and mesas seemed much smaller than he had ever known them. A hawk glided lazily by, seeming to give a start of surprise when it glanced in Omaha's direction. Omaha could see the land below changing quickly. He was moving much faster than a man on horseback could ever hope to. A river had slipped into view. It could only be the San Juan, and up ahead were the Goosenecks. His course had altered to a bit more northerly, and Omaha took the natural shift in his direction to mean that now he would have some control over his course. Wind whistled in his ears as he swung the weight of his body left then right in an attempt to choose his own direction. Ineffectually he swayed beneath the wings he had fashioned, causing them to tilt and himself to drift crazily sideways, but not seriously altering his course to bring himself around and headed back toward the lost peak of El Capitan. What, Omaha wondered, would the boy, Little Thunder, tell the tribe if he did not come back? It would indeed be a strange tale. The boy had seen him drift on the wind, seen him still airborne disappear from view.

Again Omaha swung his body, trying to keep the wings tilted in one direction long enough to alter course against the wind, but again he was thwarted as the wind played with him along its currents as if he were no more than a bit of straw being carried along on a spring breeze. He could do nothing even to bring himself down. Although Omaha had not foreseen these problems he remained confident that there was a solution to be found, and as soon as the wind deposited him somewhere he would find it. The men of his tribe would soar like eagles, cover more ground than a man on a horse in many days, hunt on unlimited ranges, and experience the freedom of the bird in flight, if only he could figure out how to get down without getting himself killed.

Omaha felt his path dipping slightly as the Goosenecks, the twisting double curves of San Juan Canyon, opened beneath him in a spectacular abyss. He had traveled before inside the walls of the canyon, but no man before him had ever seen the gray misty walls of the canyon from this angle. The wind seemed almost to suck him down into the canyon as he drifted lower, following the curves of the snakelike twists of the canyon through no action of his own. Drifting and soaring, he wondered how long it would be before his feet again touched the ground, or if he was fated to meet his end, smashed against a brooding canyon wall where it rose from the river far below.

As the wind swept him along at speeds that gained and lost momentum almost as if he were being passed from one invisible giant's hand to another, Omaha spotted movement in the canyon below. Almost as if by request the pulsing wind dropped him a bit closer to the flowing river and he saw a lone man more clearly as the rider made haste in a generally westerly direction. Omaha did not have the chance to observe his movements long as the wind snatched him beyond a jutting canyon wall, where it took another hairpin turn and lost the lone rider to his sight. But, a little farther on, it gave him something else to see. A small band of Indians was making its way along the same river's edge as the lone rider he had spotted. Moving at his speed and height it was impossible for Omaha to tell which was looking for which, if indeed either was.

Behind Omaha, moving along the canyon floor, the lone rider, stocky and hunched in his saddle, caught a fleeting glimpse of Omaha's shadow as he passed overhead. Glancing skyward, the old scout had expected to see a huge bird drifting majestically on outstretched wings. What he did see was Omaha Jones dipping and wheeling uncontrollably on air currents that changed with alarming speed within the canyon's walls. In another instant the strange vision was lost to his sight, plucked from view by the fickle wind that toyed with the flying man. It was just as well. The old scout had not been prepared to believe what he had seen anyway.

The band of Indians were of a different attitude. One of their number chancing to glance skyward had spotted Omaha as he swooped down on them, careening crazily toward a rock wall. Drawing the attention of the other Indians to the spectacle, they had stared, awe-struck, as Omaha Jones drifted across their patch of blue sky. They knew what they had seen and they did not question it. It was an omen, a sign of some kind. The tribe's medicine man would know what it meant when they got back to him with the news. They would have attempted to follow Omaha's progress, but the canyon walls were steep, and they would not have been able to find a trail to the top before he was lost to their sight in the distance. Besides, none could predict the direction he would take next with enough accuracy to suggest setting out in pursuit.

For his part, Omaha had lost interest in what was transpiring on the ground below. Suddenly, at breathtaking speed, the wind was sweeping him along and a gray, mist-shrouded wall loomed before him. The wind that was propelling him forward was not lifting as well, and he did not have enough height to clear the canyon wall that swung toward him with what was, to Omaha, astonishing speed. Grimacing, he instinctively closed his eyes seconds before he should have slammed into the solid rock that barred his further flight.

Without warning the wind lifted from below, and as if he had been launched from a springboard, he was jerked almost straight up in the air, the coolness of the exposed rock brushing his legs. Omaha's eyes popped open at the close proximity of the earth to his feet and automatically he reached for it, stretching, but the wind filled his wings, and once again he was soaring upward, unable to fight the powerful lift of the wind with only the weight of his body. He had become no more than a plaything to the wind and he was beginning to believe he had designed the strange-shaped wings suspended above him too well. Were the gods he had prayed to having a little game at his expense?

The terrain was changing again as he was

12

swept speedily along, now more in an easterly direction. Occasionally the San Juan River leapt into view and then was lost again to sight as either he or the winding river changed course. Once past the Goosenecks, Omaha found himself soaring above country that was unfamiliar to him and he was beginning to lose track of how far he had managed to travel on his wings.

Time was passing quickly, the sun was nearing a position in the crystal blue sky almost directly overhead and Omaha Jones was glad he had extended the curve in the wings well beyond his head, providing him with protection against the blazing sun. Below, the land seemed to be rising, pitched toward the distant Rockies he had passed through only twice in his life. Once on the way to school in the East, and again on his journey back home. He had never roamed the land, prowled the mountains, but it was becoming apparent that he was now going to have the opportunity he had passed up several years before, providing he did not wind up dead.

As he watched, the land below broke into green rolling foothills and rough gullies. A camp of some kind, a collection of shacks and tents, burst into view from the shelter of a clump of trees for a moment, then Omaha sped on. To his eagle's-eye view the hillside opened into a green arena, and he was low

13

enough to make out the fact that two women were fighting. Around them was a scattering of men, some of whom appeared to be cheering on the fight while others were trying to put an end to the dispute as it rolled and tumbled its way across the stretch of green grasses. Omaha would have liked to see the outcome of the fight himself, but already air currents were carrying him on. Craning his neck, he tried to keep sight of what was transpiring below as long as he could. As he did, the huge shadow of his wings slipped soundlessly over the gathering below.

Abruptly, one head jerked skyward, followed by another and another. Their faces gleamed palely from beneath the shadows of their hats as heads tipped far back in an effort to see more clearly. Still struggling together against the carpet of green, the women were entirely forgotten as the men surrounding them jabbed each other, gesticulating wildly as the man-bird drifted slowly overhead. A few broke formation from where they had been gathered about the women and started to run after the peculiar sight that was drifting across their line of vision.

In another few moments, the rest of the crowd followed the leaders, hotfooting it after the stranger who sailed the skies, leaving the women alone and to their own devices. At the loss of their audience the pair of scrapping women paused, each locked in the grip of the other as they gazed toward the sky at what had so completely stolen the attention from them. Far to the east, getting smaller against the blueness of the sky as the men continued to thunder after it, was what looked to be a man, hanging suspended in the air beneath a pair of rigidly outstretched wings. Within minutes all was silent. All the men had disappeared into the far hills trying to get themselves a better look, and the women sat in the grass, their clothes and hair in disarray, staring after the spot that grew smaller in the distance with each passing second.

Far below him, Omaha could see the men rushing after him as a herd, holding onto their hats, stumbling over tufts of thick, tall grass, and challenging low rock-strewn hills at breakneck speed in their attempts to keep up with his progress. Had he been closer to the ground, Omaha would have considered calling out to them for help. They seemed like a stalwart lot. Had he been lower, perhaps ... But he was not, and the wind carried him on.

Omaha Jones was tired, and the air around him was growing rapidly colder. His outstretched arms cried out for release though he was able to relieve the strain a bit by shifting his weight back and forth against the leather thongs that bound him securely

15

in. Had it not been for the additional broad leather thongs that added support beneath his arms like a sling, Omaha was sure he would have collapsed in sheer exhaustion by now. The sun was well past its zenith, and the ground below in its overall contour continued to rise toward the peaks that loomed now in the distance. A cabin, sheltered within a clump of trees, popped into view and again Omaha could make out tiny figures of people moving about below. This time it was only two that he had seen and he was sure they could not have seen him in that fleeting moment.

Omaha Jones was wrong. Wrapped in a daydream, Cinnamon Clayton had been gazing up at the vast empty expanse of clear blue the instant Omaha passed overhead. Startled, she blinked for an instant, but then accepted it as if it were a commonplace occurrence.

'Cinnamon!' a low gruff voice snapped her name. 'Cinnamon, get on back here with that firewood I sent you to fetch.'

'I just saw a man drifting across the sky,' Cinnamon said dreamily as he walked up to her. 'He had wings just like a bird!'

'Quit yore yarn spinnin' and get yourself back to the cabin,' the man said with exasperation, grabbing her by the arm and dragging her only mildly protesting back to the cabin door.

Pulling against the hand that gripped her tightly Cinnamon paused there, gazing over her shoulder and yearning to share the open blue sky with the man she had seen passing overhead. To glide on the wind with the freedom of a bird.

Arms numb and unfeeling, Omaha continued on his enforced journey. He had long since lost all track of distance and had no idea as to how far he had come since the San Juan's Goosenecks. The cabin and the last people he had spotted had been left far behind. Wind carried him along on gusts and pauses, but the air was much cooler and the earth seemed to be rising faster than the moving air could carry him aloft. There was no longer the lift to the sweep of the wind and gradually he was coming lower, easing down toward the earth that he longed to plant his feet once again firmly upon.

Pine trees covered the rising hills, and great masses of earth lurched suddenly heavenward in Omaha's path. The cluster of peaks he had seen rising in the distance when the sun had been high overhead were quickly looming up before him to bar his path. Now he was certain he would have to come down. The wind could not possibly lift him over the mountains that rose before him. Although Omaha Jones had set out to prove a point, he had never expected to go on proving it for so many hours.

17

Snow began appearing on the rough ground in small patches. It was spring, but Omaha had reached the high places and here snow sometimes fell late. Like an ice bath, cold air washed over him, and suddenly he was losing altitude fast. The sun, now behind him and just over his right wing, winked in his side vision as his wings dipped and lurched as he dropped quickly earthward. Omaha gave a wild yip of exultation, and then he saw the slope and stand of pines he was headed for instead of open ground.

CHAPTER TWO

With a start, Omaha realized his course was taking him birdlike directly for the trees that towered ahead. It almost seemed their green limbs spread out like a vast network of snares, and that had taken root there many years ago for the sole purpose of snagging him now. Quickly the wind carried him forward on a chilled gust, but he continued to drop with surprising speed. The trees rising up out of the mountainside ahead, a huddled green mass, became more individual and distinct with each passing second.

In a frenzy, Omaha tried to work with his wings again, swinging his weight madly from

18

side to side in an attempt to alter his course enough to swing clear of the trees into the spot of a clearing he had spied off to the south. The world tilted crazily, swinging away from him in broad arcs as Omaha tipped the wings on the wind that propelled him. He swayed like a toy on the end of a giant's string, but there was no escaping the wall of green trees that rushed toward him.

Cringing, Omaha blinked, then somehow managed to explode with a savage war whoop instead of the shriek of surprise that welled up in his throat as the limbs of a towering pine reached out to snatch him from the sky with a grip like a wildcat, scratching, poking and jabbing him in every quarter as the mighty tree jerked and limbs swayed under the impact. He heard the sharp snap of something breaking and the soft popping sounds that could only be holes opening in the finely worked leather skin of his wings. Swaying gently on the springy limbs, he hung there, the cold mountain air biting into him as the wind that had carried him so far, now swept around him, touching his bruised and cut body here and there, like the soft gentle fingers of a lover. Like a trussed-up chicken Omaha hung there and he knew he was in trouble. There was no one to cut him loose. Had he reached the valley floor as planned and been unable to get free himself, Little Thunder would have done the job. He would have had a long wait for the young brave to climb down from El Capitan, but were he to wait for him here it would be even longer.

For a moment Omaha preferred to ignore his situation and kept his eyes closed as his wild swaying motion amongst the sturdy limbs slowed. The white half of him swore with a broad vocabulary. The half that was Sioux was a bit more philosophical about his position. He could have been killed. Being so far from home, his disappearance would have been shrouded in mystery, the knowledge of his flight taken with him to his ancestors. He was ruminating over the fact that he had no desire to join his ancestors, red or white, as yet when he heard the sound.

It was not the wind, or his own movements among the branches as his feet, dangling free, sought instinctively to gain some kind of solid purchase. It was a sound he had heard before, but never so close that he could almost feel the hot breath blasting in his face. An icy chill of fear ran up Omaha's spine though in fact he was a brave man, and his piercing gray eyes shot open and locked with a pair of golden orbs blazing anger, fear, and hatred only a few feet away.

With disbelief Omaha stared at the enraged mountain lion that shared his tree. The great tawny cat was perched on a stout limb close to the main trunk, ears laid back, a gleaming snarl curling its lips. For whatever reason, the animal was treed, and for Omaha that meant this animal could be in only the worst kind of temper. Hung up to dry like last week's laundry, his feet pedaling empty air, his wings wedged into the tree's branches at a cockeyed angle, Omaha took a deep slow breath, his eyes never leaving the cat's. Long ago his daddy had told him a man could stare down any animal if he had guts enough, and the Indians looked upon the wild animals as their brothers. Omaha just hoped that his brother in the tree did not have it in mind to disembowel him. With his knife in its sheath strapped to his leg, and his arms still firmly attached to the wings, there was nothing Omaha could do to stop it.

With only his voice for a weapon, Omaha started to yell at the cat as he had once heard his father take on a marauding bear with his rifle empty. Omaha used his most authoritative voice, concentrating on the sound of it more than the words he was uttering as his eyes never left those of the mountain lion.

'Get back!' Omaha blasted the animal verbally. 'Get your hide and bones down out of this tree!' he commanded as a growl rumbled through the big cat that faced him, and saliva dripped from the exposed teeth. 'Get back,' Omaha ordered again though

21

there was nowhere else for the mountain lion to go except back down the tree, something the cat plainly did not intend to do, though it did seem to cringe back tighter against the tree trunk before Omaha's onslaught.

Pressing his small advantage, Omaha continued to berate the enraged and now thoroughly confused animal. Its golden eyes still mirrored hate and anger, but some bewilderment appeared to be there as well. Not planning on letting the big cat regain the upperhand in the situation, Omaha opened his mouth to let forth another volley when a voice thundered from far below.

'What kind of damn fool trick you trying to pull? Get the hell down out of that tree and away from my cat! Been trackin' that devil cat for days,' he bellowed.

Before Omaha could answer the disembodied voice or hurl another invective in the cat's direction, the cougar tensed, almost seeming to come off the limb at the sound of the voice issuing from below. With a vicious snarl the enraged cat took a swipe at Omaha with one mighty paw. Omaha saw it coming. With a gasp he sucked in his chest and stomach before the cat's ripping swipe of claws. Like hot irons, Omaha felt them pass over his left arm and halfway across his chest. The leather thongs that bound Omaha's left arm to the wing fell away as if they had been no more than the most

22

delicate of sewing thread and bright crimson blood sprang forth in the furrows left in his skin by the claws.

Omaha smelled the closeness of the big cat, felt the soft brush of the animal's fur as it passed almost directly over him at an impossible angle. From the base of the quivering pine there rose a gravel-voiced barrage of colorful swearwords that could have peeled the bark off the tree.

An instant later the cat was gone, having leapt over Omaha to a sturdy branch in the next tree. With astounding speed, the cougar descended it and was off across a clearing at a cross-country lope. Omaha did not see it go, and he did not care which direction it had taken. Freed from the thongs that had bound him, Omaha dropped from the wings' structure and hung crazily from the one arm still bound tightly in place as the blood welled up and trickled warmly down his arm and chest. The places where the cat had caught him were no more than scratches, but Omaha could still feel his heart thumping wildly inside his chest.

The swearing from beneath the tree rose in volume as the cat disappeared entirely from view. Unable to gain any solid hold on the tree, and dangling by the one arm still affixed to the wings, Omaha was doing some swearing of his own. Half free, he was now able to reach the knife in its sheath attached to his leg, but there still remained the problem of his location. He could not even think of cutting himself free until he could gain a more solid grip on some part of the tree he was wedged in. A fall from this height could be not only painful, but downright disastrous. And there were his wings to think about. They were damaged, it was true, but Omaha did not think they were beyond repair.

Far below, the swearing had finally stopped, though Omaha could still hear sounds of movement and knew whoever it was down below, had not left. A long silent pause dragged on, during which the sun continued to speed toward the end of the day, threatening Omaha's already precarious position with the cloak of darkness.

'Hey,' the voice called gruffly from the base of the tree, 'you aimin' to stay up there all night?' Another long pause was punctuated by some soft scuffing sounds in the earth far below. The man on the ground could not see what was going on so high in the tree, but he called again, 'I don't hold losin' my cat agin ya'. Could use a little company if you're a mind to join me. Don't get many visitors up here.'

As the sun drifted lower in the western sky, threatening momentarily to duck behind some distant hills, the air was getting much cooler fast and Omaha could feel the bumps rising along his flesh in response to the sudden chill. Unsure of the man below, a stranger to him, Omaha was hesitant to admit the true situation he found himself in, but it was evident he was going to have to do something, or in fact spend the night in the chilling mountain cold, hanging from a pine tree. His arm, he decided, could not take it. There was not enough daylight left to make a studied, rational decision.

'I'd be pleased to join you,' Omaha called down, 'but I'm stuck.'

'Stuck!' the voice thundered from below. 'You pullin' my leg? How kin you be stuck in a tree? You climbed up, didn't you? Climb down the way you climbed up.' Though the bulky man at the base of the tree peered upward expectantly he could see nothing of the man high in the branches of the tree who spoke to him. The limbs were too thick with needles and the shadows of approaching evening cast a mottled blanket of blackness over everything above.

'It's not that easy,' Omaha parried, and though he hated to admit his next statement, he said it anyway. 'I could sure use a hand.'

'A hand!' the disembodied voice demanded gruffly. 'You want me to climb that there tree along with you!?' He craned his neck again, trying to see up into the tree.

'It's the only way I'm going to get down.' Omaha tried to sound matter-of-fact about the situation.

Again the long pause from below, then the return of the gravel voice. 'I ain't one to leave a man in a fix if I can help, but I warn you, boy, if I haul myself up there and there ain't one hell of a good reason, I'll throw you off the top of this here tree myself.'

Omaha Jones did not think that statement needed an answer, so he kept his silence as he heard the other man begin to climb. There was a lot of heaving, grunting, and the sharp snapping of small branches as the plainly heavy man made his way up among the branches, working his way with surprising speed toward Omaha's position. Omaha struggled to make his predicament look a little more dignified for when the head would pop through the branches, but there was just no escaping the fact that he was hanging awkwardly by one arm from a contraption of strange design, and was marked crimson by the cat the gravel-voiced hunter had been after. Occasionally a small pine branch would flip across his face, making it difficult for him to concentrate on anything else.

Dusk was beginning to settle over the mountains by the time the huge hulk of a man climbed high enough to lock eyes with Omaha. When he did, there was a long moment as each regarded the other. Then, the tanned, seamed face broke into hearty peals of laughter that almost toppled him from his perch. Yellowed teeth showed plainly where the heavy gray-streaked beard split with his laughter, and his hawklike green eyes never left the dangling Omaha.

'What the hell kind of half-breed stunt you trying to pull?' the broad beefy bear of a man demanded, discerning the roots of Omaha's origin almost instantly.

With hastily stifled anger, Omaha eyed the man stiffly. He needed the man's help at the moment and it would not be wise to rile him. Besides, while Omaha had heard the derogatory term of half-breed used often enough before with venom, coming from this man the tone had sounded almost like an affectionate term of endearment. Omaha eyed the big man, made to seem even bigger by virtue of the heavy pelts that hung about his shoulders in layers that he had not bothered to remove for the climb. There was a hard, lantern jaw hidden beneath the bush of a beard, and a roman nose jutted out above. Green eyes glittered from beneath thick wiry eyebrows of dull brown, and his head was topped by a thatch of ragged cut red-brown hair.

'Name's Grizzly Tanner,' he offered, sliding forward on a stout branch that bowed beneath his bulk. 'Most folks though call me Griz.'

'Omaha Jones,' Omaha responded

27

quickly, all too aware of the dusk rolling across the land in the sun's wake as it set.

'Omaha,' Griz mused to himself, pausing. 'Ain't that Sioux?'

Not exactly eager for conversation, Omaha was eager to get down from his undesirable perch, so he nodded tolerantly in Griz's direction.

At the sight of Omaha dangling from his wings Griz chuckled softly. 'What kind of damn fool contraption is that?' he demanded, getting a full view of the wings wedged into the branches as he worked his way forward. 'Why'd ya' want to climb all the way up here with that hanging on your back? And dressed thataway to boot?' he nodded toward Omaha's ceremonial leggings and breechclout.

Omaha's patience was wearing thin, and as far as he could tell Griz Tanner was in no hurry to get on with what he had come up the huge pine to do. It seemed as if the old hunter was enjoying himself. Sitting back, he was balancing on a branch, eyeing Omaha with cool detachment.

'I didn't climb up,' Omaha said a bit tightly. 'I flew. And now I'm in kind of a hurry to get down from here, so how about giving me a hand?'

Griz did not look particularly startled by Omaha's statement. Either he did not believe him, or he just plain did not care. He

28

grinned at Omaha, forcing out the thoughtful frown that had marked his leathery forehead.

'Just hold your horses, boy,' Griz said amiably. 'I got to do me some thinking. You've got yourself in between a rock and a hard place there. If I just cut you down, I'll probably drop you on your head. 'Sides, I can't see what you're in such a rush about. Seems to me if you hadn't scared the daylights out of my cat you might'a been hanging around up here by yourself for days,' he pointed out shrewdly. 'Fact is, I sometimes don't come by here for weeks.'

He stared at Omaha a bit longer, eyeing the set of the wings and the odd angle at which his body hung from them. 'Flew up here, you say?' Griz questioned. 'Couldn't you just fly back down were I to give you a push out of here?'

'No!' Omaha answered sharply. 'The tree did some damage to the wings. I'd drop like a rock.'

Griz nodded sagely. 'Tell you what I'll do. I'll pull that there branch down to your free hand there, then cut the other one loose. You should be able to work your way in to the trunk then.'

Without waiting for Omaha's acceptance or rejection of his proposal Griz heaved himself upward upon the branch he had crawled away from the massive tree trunk

29

on, and balancing precariously, reached up above his own head to snag a firm hold on a springy higher branch. With deceptive ease he pulled it downward, settling himself again on the stouter branch and guiding the more slender limb to Omaha's outstretched hand. Omaha was a little nervous about the situation, but he had to admit that he could see no other way to go about accomplishing his end. He got a good tight hold on the more slender branch, hoping it would hold when it bore his full weight after Griz cut the last of the leather thongs that still bound him to his wings.

A knife flashed in Griz's hand as he leaned forward to slash the thongs that bound Omaha. The razor-sharp knife slipped through the tough rawhide thongs as if through a fresh cooked noodle. What followed happened so fast, Griz hardly had time to suck his breath in through one of the holes in his mouth where a tooth had been with a quavering whistle before Omaha Jones was lost to his sight.

Instead of bowing down beneath his weight as both Omaha and Griz had expected, the limb Griz had handed him sprung suddenly upward as Omaha was released from his bondage, taking him with it like a sparrow on a high wind. The wings, torn loose from their roost among the branches, slid suddenly sideways and launched themselves into an awkward glide to the ground. Griz heard them hit the earth, but with night settling in quickly, it was impossible for him to see anything beyond a few feet below, or above him. Trees moaned and whispered as they swayed gently in the stirring of the night air, and after Omaha's unexpected launch those were the only sounds moving through the trees. Though Griz listened closely for some kind of movement from above, there was nothing but silence.

'Boy,' he called out. 'You all right, boy?!' Only silence answered him, and Griz tried again. 'Now, you answer me, boy!' he demanded. 'I ain't had no company of any kind up here for months, maybe longer. And I don't cotton none to the idea of hauling your carcass down out of here to go bury it somewhere, so you best answer me!'

Overhead, Omaha, wedged in between some slender limbs as if he had been shot from the ground arrowlike, grunted in reply and swayed with the tree limbs as the air stirred them. For long seconds he had been dazed by the sudden and sharp contact of his head with a limb overhead. He had heard the rumble of Griz's voice, but not understood the words. With an effort he roused himself fully, realizing he was still tightly clutching the limb Griz had handed him. With an oath he released it.

31

'You stuck again, boy!' Griz called up.

'No,' Omaha grated, edging his way through the slender, spidery limbs near the crown of the tree toward the trunk.

'I'll see you down below then,' Griz growled amiably as he started to descend the tree trunk, raising enough of a commotion for Omaha to compare him to his namesake. The only difference was, a full-grown grizzly could not climb trees.

The big man moved with surprising agility and speed. Omaha could hear him quickly making his way down the tree, the sounds fading as he got further along. Not having seen or heard his wings' unfortunate independent descent, Omaha looked for them on his way down, not able to gauge exactly where they had been lodged in the tree after his bone-jarring jerk to a higher elevation.

Inching his way down the rough tree trunk, Omaha peered continuously in amongst the tangled branches, searching vainly for some sign of his wings. One searching foot touched the soft carpet of pine needles that covered the ground before Omaha realized he had come all the way down without locating the precious wings. He was about to scale the tree again, in the dark, when he spotted a bulky figure approaching through the gloom, toting something that was obviously not very heavy.

In another moment, Omaha could make out the vague shape of his wings in the gloom.

'Figured you might be wanting these,' Griz said as he made out Omaha's form at the base of the tree.

Omaha nodded his thanks solemnly and took the damaged wings from Griz's grasp as the moon rose above them, splashing the area in a soft dim light.

Griz stared at Omaha as if seeing him for the first time, then shook his head. 'That's what you get when you go messing with a she-cougar,' he said in observation of Omaha's numerous scratches and bruises. 'You oughtn't to tease them cats like that.' Then he noted in a serious tone, 'Why, you ain't even dressed proper for this weather.' Peeling off one of the pelts that hung about his broad shoulders, Griz threw it over Omaha's naked ones. 'You must be plum loco, boy.' He gave a wave of his hand. 'Come on, we best get on back to the dugout.'

For the moment, Omaha was willing to go where Griz led. With the sun set, there was an icy bite to the air that even the pelt Griz had given him did not do much to ward off. As they walked, patches of snow crunched beneath Omaha's moccasins. The wings were easy to carry along. They had not nearly so much lift to them now that they were punctured with so many rips and holes.

33

But at least the framework was intact. With that, Omaha knew it would not be difficult to repair them.

They trudged on, Griz setting a brisk pace as if he were now suddenly in a hurry to get back to the dugout. Omaha did not mind the pace, in spite of the fact that he was carrying the sometimes unwieldy wings. It stirred his blood and warmed him. They walked along like that for a long way, Griz in the lead, and Omaha following a short way behind, not really paying much attention, just following the course the old hunter took, until Griz disappeared abruptly from sight.

Omaha blinked, not able to believe his eyes. One instant, Griz was there, several yards ahead of him, the next there was no sign of him. Omaha stopped, puzzled. There was a moon. It was not reasonable to suppose that he had somehow passed Griz by in the darkness. A moment later a low chuckle rumbled up to greet Omaha, and a large, rough hand snagged his wrist, pulling him down into what appeared to be nothing more than pitch darkness. Omaha released his hold on the wings as he staggered blindly forward, too taken by surprise to resist as total darkness enveloped him. An instant later a heavy wooden door swung outward, opening to a square of light that led to the dugout's interior.

Griz chuckled again. 'It's just a little joke

of mine, boy.' He spread his arms expansively. 'Welcome!'

CHAPTER THREE

Inside, the dugout was snug against the icy chill of the night. Its construction was almost cavelike, and Griz dropped to one knee to stir up the still glowing embers of an earlier fire, stoking it high until a roaring blaze crackled in the fireplace that was set in one wall, using a natural hole in the top of the earthen dugout to allow the smoke to escape. From end to end the dugout was not much more than ten feet across. That included the pitched sides where a man would have to be on his knees to fit inside. The roof was low, and the wall where the fireplace sat, rough with rocks and bits of long-buried sticks protruding out into the room. The flatter of the rocks Griz used for shelves, and the stouter of the bits of wood for pegs. A scattering of canned foods, flour, salt, and coffee were on the rock shelves, and from the pegs hung a couple of heavy frying pans. Apparently all the clothing to Griz's name, one extra shirt, pair of pants, and hat, were also hung there. A coffeepot occupied a round flat rock beside the fireplace and several stumps were set around the dugout, polished smooth from much sitting. Animal pelts were piled in one corner close to the stout bunk Griz had built along the wall that curved away from the fireplace.

The place was well concealed. Omaha had had no inkling as to its presence before Griz had dragged him down the slope into the darkness. He was curious to see the place's location by the light of day. At night there was no way it could be found unless a man knew exactly where it was, or stumbled upon it purely by accident.

Satisfied with the fire he had built, though it scarcely touched the gloom of the opposite wall, Griz flashed Omaha a broad grin and rummaged about in a pile of animal furs before coming up with a stoneware jug. Sitting cross-legged before the fire, the pelt Griz Tanner had thrown over his shoulders earlier still in place, Omaha had barely felt the chill begin to leave his bones when Griz thrust the jug toward him.

'Here, take a slug of that!' Griz beamed, uncorking the jug as Omaha accepted it.

Tossing his head back, Omaha took a deep draught of the mixture and felt it begin to burn a trail down his throat to his stomach. He fought back the choking sensation that rose in his throat by taking a second, smaller drink.

Griz laughed, raising the jug to his own lips. 'It's my own stuff,' he commented with a smack of his lips as he lowered the jug, then raised it again for a longer pull. 'Here, have some more.'

Omaha obliged, liking the feeling that washed over him. Having had nothing to eat since early morning, the alcohol was affecting him quickly. Griz's brew went down easier this time, its taste having had time to grow on him. He took another drink, then returned the jug to Griz.

'Do much trapping?' Omaha asked as they continued to drink.

Griz shook his head. 'No more'n what I can eat and feed my friend over there.' He waved vaguely toward a dark corner. 'Just never waste nothing. Would even keep a skunk pelt were I to eat me a skunk.'

Omaha focused his gaze in the direction Griz indicated, but saw only the pile of furs he had noticed earlier. 'What friend?' he asked, suppressing a hiccup.

'My friend. Ezra.' Griz again gestured toward the corner, the strong jug whiskey clearly beginning to have an effect on him as well. 'Over yonder. He makes more of a to-do when I come in alone. Don't care for strangers much. They mostly want to give him a good kick or maybe shoot him.'

Puzzled, Omaha again returned his blurring gaze to the dark corner. He stared intently at the pile of pelts for long seconds, but saw nothing. Then, abruptly, something started to move. Staring a bit longer, he realized with a start that one of the pelts was alive. And beneath it was a coyote. The animal was stretched out full length amongst the pelts, half buried in them. Omaha had assumed his pelt to be one of many.

'That's your friend?' Omaha asked in disbelief, accepting the jug again from Griz's hand.

Griz nodded, half reclining on the dirt floor. 'Been with me ever since I kilt his mama by accident few years back. Didn't know she had a cub when she come raiding my camp after sundown.' There was a sadness to Griz's face as he again took the jug back from Omaha, taking a long deep pull from its neck. 'Found Ezra wanderin' around alone next morning, so I kept him. He don't eat much,' Griz ended by way of explanation.

At the second mention of his name Ezra rose from the pile of furs, stretched and ambled over to plunk himself down beside Griz with an expansive yawn.

'Usually folks don't care much for coyotes,' Griz said, fondling an ear the beast had positioned conveniently close to his reach, 'but me, I like 'em. They don't put on no airs like some folks. Go through life being just what they are, leaning to the sneaky side. I like breeds for a lot of the same reasons,' Griz offered by way of a compliment. 'Crafty devils,' he said almost in awed wonderment.

'Only got one other friend in these mountains,' Griz went on after he took another generous pull from the jug. He paused a moment, then said, 'And that's Emily.'

Raising a quizzical eyebrow, Omaha again accepted the now sloshing jug Griz offered. He had gotten used to Griz's warm, back-handed references to Indians on the whole and half-breeds like himself in particular. He was more interested in the man's comment about Emily. He did not ask the obvious question, but instead drank deeply of the liquor and waited for the big man's explanation, which was sure to come without any coaxing.

'Emily is my hoss,' Griz said finally, his words thickened by the whiskey they were consuming.

Omaha nodded somberly. He could grasp that. Men alone in the mountains often thought of their horses or mules as their friends. They depended on each other. And, as Griz did not expand the subject further, Omaha assumed that such was the case of Grizzly Tanner.

'You live with the Sioux much?' Griz asked abruptly, changing the subject as his ability to focus diminished in direct proportion to the amount of the jug whiskey he consumed.

Nodding, Omaha almost fell over as he threw his head back for yet another drink. It occurred to him to notice that they were both getting pleasantly drunk, but he had categorized Grizzly Tanner earlier and decided he was in good company.

'Lived with the Sioux most of my life, off and on, before I went to school back East awhile. Wintered with them when my father was alive, lived with them when my mother went back to the tribe after he died.' The whiskey made Omaha feel expansive, like he wanted to talk, though ordinarily he was not one for saying much. 'Went to school with some money my father had saved in a St Louis bank. When I got back everything was changed. Many old friends were dead in battles fought with the whites.'

'Redskins,' Griz muttered philosophically as he slid off the stump to join Omaha on the earth floor, 'always rapin' and pillagin'...'

Omaha shook his head in a slow negative arc.

'Lookee here, boy, you tellin' me you ain't never raped or pillaged?'

'Have you?' Omaha demanded, a hurt look flashing across his face.

Griz shook his head, grasping the stone jug by its stubby neck. 'Give some occasional thought to it though,' he said with a wicked grin.

Omaha gave him a sour look. 'I am not

40

interested in wars and battles. I want only to fly like the eagle. I have already proved it can be done. You yourself helped me out of the tree I landed in.'

'Won't work,' Griz said positively as he wiped his mouth on his sleeve. 'You want something to eat?' he asked a little belatedly, climbing unsteadily to his feet to swing a big pot of beans and meat out over the fire that burned hot in the fireplace.

Omaha nodded and sat back numbly, the jug sitting at a cockeyed angle beside him, but spilling none of its remaining contents. 'Why won't it work?' he asked at last, the full impact of Griz's first statement sinking in for the first time.

' 'Cause,' Griz answered simply, 'if the maker of this here earth either red or white had meant for man to fly, he would have given him wings like that there eagle you're talking about.' On unsteady legs, Griz got out a couple of hollowed-out wooden bowls and spoons for the beans, settling again at Omaha's side before the fire, Ezra curled up contentedly between their feet.

'If the gods had meant man to cross the mountains each year, they would have given him cloven hoofs like the bighorn and shaggy pelts like the grizzly,' Omaha snapped back, though his speech slurred and his tongue would not behave itself.

Griz let that thought wander aimlessly

through the befuddled corridors of his whiskey-fogged brain, giving it long consideration. Then coming up with no comeback for it, reverted to his time-honored tradition of changing horses in midstream.

'Did I tell you about Emily, my hoss?' Griz asked solemnly as he turned his concentration to the task of dishing up the steaming beans.

Omaha looked blank for a moment, the overabundance of whiskey making his usually nimble mind do a double take at Griz's abrupt change in topic. 'You started to,' he remembered. 'Said she was your horse. You been riding her long?'

Griz frowned and stuck out his lower lip. 'Don't ride her at all. But,' he added with a broad wink, 'there's folks I let that do.'

Puzzled at the remark, Omaha paused in mid-bite of the beans and meat mixture from his bowl. 'What good is she if *you* don't ride her?'

Griz grinned as he picked up the whiskey jug to wash down a huge mouthful of food. 'When I get to a town or some mining camp, I race her. Looks all tiny and delicate like, but she can really run. Emily goes for long distances. Ain't seen a horse yet she couldn't take on a long run. And me, I got me a old mule I ride whenever I'm of a mind to. Most I like to walk.

'I could sure use me a partner for a spell,' Griz went on, thrusting the jug that was much lighter now than when they had started, again in Omaha's direction. 'You might ride her for me if'n you were a mind to. I can guarantee you make some good money.'

Omaha started to shake his head negatively, thought better of it in deference to the dizziness that swept over him, and used instead his thickening vocal cords to respond. 'Don't think I can do it for you,' he answered, his tongue making war on his teeth as he attempted to form clear speech. 'Got to get back. Got my wings to work on. Lots of work to do,' he ended with a broad wave of his hand.

Somewhere back in the deeper reaches of his consciousness, Omaha knew he was drunk, but then so was Grizzly, and now just to keep things equal, Griz was pouring out a generous cupful of the stuff for Ezra, who sniffed the brew tentatively, then dove in like it was spring water in the desert.

'Well, hell, boy, ain't no reason why you can't do both!' Griz boomed. 'We're both gonna be headin' in the same direction anyway. What harm could it do to stop over in some town for a day or two here and there? You scratch my back and I'll scratch yours. Got some hides you might be able to use to patch up them wings of yourn.'

Peering through the alcoholic haze that enveloped all his thoughts, Omaha frowned as the words tumbled from Griz's mouth. What he was saying made sense, but that was just what was worrying Omaha. That Griz should win his point so easily made Omaha think he was even more drunk than he had first believed himself to be. What surprised Omaha even more was that he heard himself asking Griz about the proposition he had already firmly turned down in his own mind.

'What do you figure my end of this partnership would include?'

'Ridin' Emily when I got us a race set up,' Griz replied quickly. 'Maybe haulin' me back to camp should I get myself so drunk in one of them towns so as to start to fritterin' away our money. Most important of all, gettin' Emily out of town if trouble shows. Mostly the mule and me can take care of ourselves. 'Course if there's a fight and more than six or eight fellas jump me at one time you might lend a hand.' He paused. 'You kin fight bare-fisted, can't you?'

Omaha nodded.

'I was gonna pull out in a couple of weeks, but could do it in a couple a days if that'd suit you better,' Griz offered, trying to make it impossible for Omaha to say no.

To Griz's satisfaction and Omaha's surprise, he succeeded.

'All right, partner.' Omaha stuck out his

hand forcefully for Griz to shake and folded gracefully to the floor, out cold.

Griz heard Omaha agree, but did not see him pass out or hear him slide softly to the floor above his own deep throaty snores where he leaned limply against the stump where he had sat, a self-satisfied smile touching his face.

CHAPTER FOUR

When Omaha woke up the next morning, he was very careful to cautiously open just one eye at a time. Even the dim light that managed to filter in from outside sent a jab of pain through his eyes, and his head felt like a mushy, over-ripe melon. Dimly, above the intense throbbing inside his skull, Omaha could hear Griz still snoring enthusiastically where he lay half propped against the old stump, Ezra sprawled out on his side close by him.

Dragging himself slowly to his feet Omaha stood unsteadily for a moment, swaying toward the dugout's door. Wrapping the fur Griz had thrown over him closer about his naked shoulders, he braced himself for the first bite of morning air as he reached for the latch. And he got almost exactly what he had expected of the mountain morning as the door swung inward beneath his hand. Frosted air hit him like a sharp slap in the face, and for a moment it almost sent him reeling back inside the dugout. But Omaha clamped his teeth tightly shut against their chattering and plunged on ahead, looking for water. Even a small stream would have done, but what Omaha came across within a few strides of the dugout was a lake. Crystals of frost shimmered along its surface, but the hard freezes of winter were past. Omaha dropped to his knees beside the lake's shore and buried his entire aching head within the lake's icy chill. He could feel the skin along his shoulders and arms rise up in gooseflesh beneath the heavy fur pelt, but he remained as he was until breath ran out and he was forced to break the surface of the water.

When he sat back on his heels bringing his head out of the water to let tiny rivers of the icy waters run unchecked over his shoulders and arms, he found Griz Tanner sprawled near him on his belly, head submerged in the position Omaha had just abandoned. Ezra was beside him, lapping up water as fast as his long tongue could go in and out of his mouth.

Focusing on the mountains that rose all around them, Omaha tried to get his bearings, but the country was totally unfamiliar to him. Omaha had managed to cover a good piece of the country during his

46

life, but there was still an even larger hunk that he knew nothing about, and this was a part of it.

'Those there are the Trinity Peaks,' Griz volunteered when he raised his head, dripping from the lake's waters.

Omaha frowned, trying to place the named landmark, finding it fit into nothing he already knew. He had lost his bearings early in his flight except for direction, and that had altered frequently upon the whim of the wind. Even so, he was sure he had come in a mostly easterly direction with a slight northerly drift. Amongst the towering trees, in the dark, it had been impossible for Omaha to tell where he was. Now, in the daylight beside a strange lake, beneath a crystal blue sky, it was still impossible.

Griz ran a hand through his thick hair, brushing the droplets of water down his back and looked at Omaha curiously. 'Don't ya even know what territory you're in?'

Omaha shrugged as if it did not really matter. 'It's something I'll have to learn to do when I fly more often.'

'You telling me you flew them wings into one of my trees, and you don't even know where the hell you are?' Griz burst out laughing with a force that shook his whole frame. Ezra even paused in his determined lapping to glance curiously from his friend to the stranger, then resumed drinking.

47

'This here,' Griz informed him when he could control his outburst of laughter, 'is part of the San Juans in south Colorado. The New Mexico line ain't too far south from here.'

Omaha's mouth dropped open at the revelation. The miles had fallen away beneath his wings as had the hours, but never had he dreamed of having come this far. The Goosenecks, he reminded himself, he should have realized the distance he had traveled when he had recognized them. Flight became more and more of a solid reality as he pondered Grizzly's words. He was in southern Colorado just north of the New Mexican line. He would have liked to have known the miles covered, but not being familiar with the country he still knew only by words where he was located and there would be no way for him to compute the miles until he returned again to El Capitan. Even then he could not be sure. But the feat remained incredible. And he had Little Thunder as his witness to the launching from El Capitan as well as Grizzly Tanner to witness his less than graceful descent into the treetops. One day's journey by air. His excitement rose, but Omaha Jones was ever mindful of the fact that there remained much that had to be done. He had to repair the wings and launch himself again.

'C'mon partner!' Griz said expansively,

giving Omaha a slap on the back that felt as if it would jar his sensitive head loose from his shoulders. 'Let's go get us some grub.'

Omaha winced in physical discomfort as his stomach did a double flip at the mere mention of food, and the remembrance of his drunken promise to Grizzly made him cringe. There was no help for it now, he had given his word. Vaguely, he remembered something being said the night before about a horse Griz wanted him to ride that was the fastest thing ever to hit that part of the country. Omaha glanced around wondering where Griz had the animal hidden and noticed in that same instant that the dugout was nowhere in sight. He knew he had not wandered more than a few strides from the dugout's door and yet he could see nothing of it.

'Over thataway.' Griz gestured toward the rounded hump of land settled amongst a stand of thick spruce trees and the deep morning shadows, perceiving Omaha's difficulty in locating it again.

'Ezra!' Griz thundered, the night before apparently having had no lasting effect after his dip in the lake. The coyote galloped after Griz, and Omaha followed along behind, feeling more like he should be crawling the remaining distance to the dugout.

Once he had the dugout located again, Omaha stayed outside while Griz sauntered in, leaving the door wide open behind him, and stoked the fire high before putting on the coffeepot. His wings, where he had not noticed them before, were propped against the curve of the dugout, the holes in the skins letting the sunlight through in a lacy pattern upon the ground. Griz, a man totally used to doing for himself, came up with some fresh fish he probably had set a trap for in the lake the night before. And without any wasted motion he started some sourdough biscuits in another pan. Omaha, sitting on the stump where Griz split his wood, felt his stomach knot up and heard it start to growl as the smells of Griz's cooking drifted out of the dugout. It was with some surprise that he realized he was hungry after all.

Letting his eyes wander, Omaha was thinking about the work that had to be done on the wings as well as some other aspects of them he should be testing, such as a ground launching and how it could be accomplished, when his practiced eye picked out the difference in the adjoining hillock. The hangover from the night before fading into the background, Omaha climbed to his feet and strolled around its base. It was not a real rise in the earth, natural to that region, it had to have been constructed. And a first glance at the southerly exposed opening confirmed Omaha's suspicions. It was a dugout stable, and it had been constructed

50

with the utmost care. Outside there were small plants growing on the curve, and air vents hidden in low scrub brush planted there for that purpose. Inside there was cross beam support, though Omaha did not think there was much danger of a cave-in, and such precautions had not been taken in Griz's own dugout, and there was the horse. Emily. She shared her quarters with a lop-eared mule, but Omaha had eyes only for the horse.

The mare was so perfect, she was something Omaha had never expected to see actually walking around. She was small, but the way she was put together made her appear even smaller. Glistening red-brown in color, she had a broad forehead marked by a white blaze and wide, liquidy brown eyes that seemed to speak to him as he stood watching her moving gracefully about the dugout's interior. Her legs were long and slender with hoofs that gave the illusion of being no bigger than silver dollars. Her mane and tail glistened like satin from frequent brushings that only Griz could have given her. In spite of the fact that winter had just passed, Emily's neck was bowed and her head held high though most animals appeared dull of eye and coat after such a season. She was as pretty a horse as Omaha had ever seen, like something out of a vision. If she could run like Griz claimed, it was no wonder he made himself some good money at the mining camps and towns in the mountains. She was a beauty, that was true, but from looks alone, it would appear a man would be forced to carry the horse on his back instead of her carrying him. Winning a race against the strapping range ponies seemed far-fetched at first glance. It was easy to see why Griz needed a rider. With his bulk upon her frail-looking back Omaha doubted she would be able to win a race against a ground beetle.

'See you two are getting to know each other,' Griz boomed after sliding up on Omaha with a silence Omaha would have sworn was impossible in a man of his bulk. 'Grub's ready. Let's pack it on in and clear out of here.'

Omaha glanced at Griz with a start. Though the past night was somewhat blurry, he seemed to remember Griz mentioning something about pulling out in a couple of days. Now, suddenly, he gave every indication of being eager to set out that very day. In fact, that very hour. Omaha ran a couple of steps to catch up with Griz's retreating form.

'What about the work I have to do on my wings?' Omaha demanded. 'We had an agreement last night. I help you riding Emily, and you help me.'

Griz nodded enthusiastically. 'We sure do,

but hell, boy, we can work on them wings on the trail just as easily as here. No point in staying longer, snow's most gone. 'Sides,' he added as he ducked into the dugout, 'Emily needs the exercise.'

What Griz said made sense, but Omaha had the disturbing feeling that he had no control over the situation. Of course he could walk off and leave Griz, but he had given his word, and he was coming to think of Griz as a friend. Besides, it would be much more comfortable riding Emily over the intervening miles than walking, carrying the wings. They were an unwieldy invention and from what Griz had told him, there were many miles to cover. The rest of the tribe would have long given him up for dead by the time he got back whether he took time out to help Griz as he had promised or not. And it was a fact that his absence from the tribe would not cause any great grief among them. They had made it crystal clear that they did not think much of him or his ideas since he had returned from the Eastern white man's school. Maybe, he pondered, it would be best for him to walk his own trail, alone.

Following Griz inside, Omaha was met with a plate of fried fish and biscuits and settled himself on the floor, this time a bit back from the fire as the chill was rapidly leaving the air with the rising of the morning sun.

'Eat hearty, boy,' Griz admonished him, 'we'll pull out soon as I finish getting my gear together.' He made a vague gesture toward the corner where the task was already almost complete.

The flour, salt, coffee, and bacon were not on the rock shelves where they had been the night before. The change of clothes was off the pegs and a good number of the pelts were tied into a large bundle near the door. The fire box was completely filled with wood as if Griz had no intention of going anywhere and the embers of the breakfast fire were already scattered, the coffeepot left sitting on the stone warmed near the fire to keep the strong liquid hot.

Griz tossed Omaha his spare shirt though it was much too large.

'You best wear it, boy,' he said amiably. 'It'll be mighty cold you running around like you are in these mountains.'

Omaha glanced about the dugout almost in awe, and donned the shirt while still staring. When had Griz had time to do it all? He had spent only a few minutes admiring Emily. It took even the Sioux longer to break camp than Griz Tanner.

Within an hour, Griz had everything packed on the mule, including Omaha's wings, and Emily saddled for the trail. The dugout was carefully closed up, as was the shelter for the animals. Without a backwards glance from Grizzly, they pulled out, he humming a little tune to himself that sounded familiar to Omaha, who was mounted on a high-stepping Emily.

CHAPTER FIVE

Emily set out upon the trail like she knew where she was heading and would be glad to get there. They did not make many miles the first day out owing to the fact that Omaha's wings were a strange and unwieldy burden for the old mule to carry. She resented the wings bobbing in rhythm to her walk within her sight. Time and again she stopped dead, refusing to take another step. Each time Griz would stop and patiently rearrange the light but troublesome burden until the old mule would again continue on.

Omaha worked Emily only lightly beneath Griz's constant reminders that the horse had just spent most of the winter cooped up in the small dugout stable where Omaha had first seen her. Too much too fast after that could easily make her sick, possibly even kill her, and Emily was too much of a pet for Griz to allow anything like that to happen. Whenever Omaha gave her a trot or a short gentle gallop, he would be back at Griz's side within only a few minutes to satisfy him that

Emily was not being pushed too hard her first day out. For his part, Griz moved along at a steady pace that would have covered a lot of ground if it were not for the stops caused by the disgruntled mule.

It was early the morning of their third day of questionable progress when they came across the girl. She was quite alone, a fact Omaha had made sure of before they got close enough to pass any words. The question as to which had come across whom was one that would remain unanswered. The girl had been traveling in a definitely easterly direction and they due west.

When she spied them, instead of being wary as any woman alone out there possessing good sense would have done, she ran forward to meet them. Clutching a small bundle tightly, she looked like a little girl lost in the woods who had been found. The difference being she was *not* a little girl and nothing about her seemed to indicate that she was lost, or anywhere other than exactly where she wanted to be. Immediately suspicious, Omaha backed off to consider the situation, but Griz was of a more charitable nature. But then, Griz seemed always to be taking in strays, either animal or human. Omaha himself was an example of that.

His hand resting on the butt of the six-gun Griz had loaned him when they came up on

56

her, Omaha cut a strange figure in his ceremonial leggings, Griz's oversized shirt, and the six-gun strapped low on his hip. Griz had apologized to Omaha for not having another rifle around to loan him, but the six-gun was all he had and a man had to have a gun in those parts. It made no difference to Omaha what he had. The time he had spent in the white man's and red man's worlds had benefited him greatly. Omaha Jones was no stranger to the six-gun. His draw was not the fastest but it served him, and his aim was deadly accurate.

The girl, breathless and flushed, smiled trustingly at the odd pair confronting her, her blue eyes dancing with excitement. 'I'm Cinnamon,' she told them before they could ask. 'Who are you?' As she spoke she craned her neck to see around behind Griz, eyeing Omaha's wings where they were strapped on the mule's back.

Before Omaha could open his mouth to answer, Cinnamon squealed with delight, pointing a rigid finger in his direction. 'I know who *you* are!' She almost jumped up and down in her excitement. 'You're the bird man! I saw you fly over the cabin! And those'—she pointed to the wings on the mule's back—'those have to be *your* wings.'

Omaha could not help grinning at Cinnamon's exuberance. She had to have been among the people he had passed over in his path of flight. She had seen him. It crossed Omaha's mind to wonder how he had looked from the ground.

'That's Omaha Jones,' Griz answered for him, 'and me, I'm Griz Tanner, ma'am. Is there something we can do for you, you being out here all alone and all, I mean?'

'Where you heading?' Cinnamon asked brightly, but rather pointlessly. It did not matter to her where they were going, she planned on going with them and their direction was already evident.

'West,' Omaha returned, still not quite sure of the situation.

Cinnamon frowned. 'I'm heading east. Can't you two change your minds and head east? I would sure be happy of the company.'

Griz and Omaha shook their heads in unison.

Cinnamon frowned again, then perked up. 'Can I change my mind and head west?'

'It's a big country, miss,' Griz said expansively. 'Guess you got yourself a right to head in any direction you want.' Griz was encouraging her, making it plain that she would be welcome to travel with them.

Omaha had not yet decided whether he liked the idea or not, but his leanings were against it. There was no telling where Cinnamon had popped up from, but it was a sure bet that there had to be some kind of trouble dogging her heels. If they took her on, they would be asking for it. Griz was no stranger to this country. He knew the same things Omaha did, but he did not seem to worry much about them.

Cinnamon, whoever she was, had the kind of wide-eyed innocence that made Omaha nervous. Almost on the skinny side, she was slender with limp brown hair that hung down around her shoulders. Her skin was creamy and flushed easily, sending an attractive blush high into her apple cheeks. She had Griz's ear now, and Omaha was able to hear only snatches of what passed between them from where he sat astride Emily several feet away.

'I guess I do have that right,' Cinnamon was telling Griz with a bright smile. 'Now,' she began with a self-conscious half stammer, 'now that I'm free.' Her attitude changed to that of a stepped-on orphan.

'You're free all right,' Griz said gruffly. 'Ain't nobody gonna say different while I'm around.' He paused. 'There ain't nobody right close by likely to try, is there?'

'Ohhhh, nooo,' Cinnamon assured him. 'It's just that ... well ... didn't you wonder why I was out here alone?'

Griz nodded. 'Sure did, but I figured you'd get around to telling us when you were of a mind to.'

Cinnamon smiled shyly, her blue eyes awash with gratitude at Griz's understanding

59

nature, and Griz was lapping up everything the slip of a girl was dishing out like a cat going after fresh milk.

'I've got to be honest with you,' Cinnamon said to Griz in low tones. 'I'm running away from a man. He bought me from the Indians who took me from a wagon train when I was just a tiny girl. If he catches me after running away like this he'll beat me within an inch of my life for sure.'

Griz frowned at her story. 'He'll have to go through me first.' Omaha heard the words barked out in a strident tone, and he knew they were taking on a hatful of trouble.

Turning to Omaha, Griz grinned. 'Looks like we got us a new partner, partner.'

Omaha smiled vaguely, feeling a bit sick inside, and nodded. There was no help for it. What it boiled down to was the fact that they could not leave her alone out there anyway. Neither he nor Griz would have the lack of conscience for it. Whatever she had said to Griz had convinced him beyond a doubt that they were doing the right thing in taking her along. It was just as well, Omaha mused, that he had not heard a word that had passed between them clearly.

'Oh, good!' Cinnamon's blue eyes lit up. 'Wait a minute.' She threw the words over her shoulder as she disappeared among the trees and thick brush.

A moment later she reappeared mounted

60

on a scrubby horse. 'Let's go,' she said eagerly.

'He yours?' Griz asked, eyeing the horse as if he had never seen such an animal before.

'Well,' Cinnamon admitted, 'I sort of had to take him when I ran away.'

Omaha slapped one hand over his face and groaned. Horse stealing was about the worst thing a person could do in this kind of country. It was the unforgivable sin.

'Don't worry, I left him another one.' Cinnamon was addressing Griz. 'I wouldn't leave a man on foot, even one I hate,' she added with the expression of an angel lighting her fair face.

Groaning again, Omaha reined Emily around to scout ahead a bit. He had a gut feeling they were going to need a good scout for their party, and he was the best among them no matter what Griz thought to the contrary. Plenty of men in that territory would be more determined to get a horse back than a woman. And not only had this woman stolen a horse, no matter how noble her cause, but she had also left the injured party another mount to follow on. The fact that she had been headed east and they west was something more to consider. Where exactly had she come from? If she were going east, then it was logical to assume whoever she was running from, and Omaha was sure she had to be running from someone, was probably behind her, to the west ... the direction they were heading in now. For the moment Omaha had no desire to pursue the thought any further. It occurred to him to wonder how he kept getting himself in deeper when all he wanted to do was construct a pair of manageable wings and fly. His was a worthy effort. The rest of what went on were merely side issues, distractions.

Emily jumped into a brisk trot with little urging from Omaha. Something he had discovered about the small horse from their first day together was her sensitivity to commands. She responded quickly and easily, her gaits more comfortable to sit than an old rocker. And now that she was loosening up after her long winter of enforced inactivity, she was constantly pushing against the bit, eager to get it between her teeth and run all out. Omaha had not let her do it yet though they had taken a couple of short runs earlier that morning. He was eager to see how fast the horse really was, but obeyed Griz's instructions to the letter. Griz wanted her brought back into shape slowly. It was Emily who had other ideas on the matter. He had to fight her most of the time now to keep her from running with the bit, and each time he pulled her up short she would shake her head irritably and snort repeatedly as if scolding him.

Omaha found a suitable campsite early and stopped to gather firewood as he waited for Griz and Cinnamon to catch up. It was near water, well screened against the chilled wind by towering spruce trees, and in consideration of the addition of their newest partner, well protected against any possible attack. Part of his agreement with Griz was that they stop each evening while there was still some daylight to enable him to work on repairing his wings. It was slow work and had to be done right so the wings would catch the wind again as they had the first time. While Omaha had taken many of his ideas from books and drawings he had seen back East in school, many of the cross pieces and supports, as well as some changes in the shape of the design were his own innovations. At least he had seen no drawings exactly like what he had come up with, and the mere fact that it had flown so far had to mean something. There were differences between the wings built by his hands and those built by others in the past. They had to have been important differences, or his design would not have succeeded where others had failed.

Omaha worked quickly with an ease born of familiarity and skill. But the whole time he busied himself with setting up the rudiments of a camp, starting a fire, stringing a picket line for the animals, and scouting the area for any varmints, two-legged or four-legged, he was aware someone was nearby. He could feel eyes upon him and he knew he was not wrong. But in the nearby vicinity of the camp he had set up, he could find no sign of anyone passing that way other than himself. Omaha would have preferred being able to pick out some sign, but the fact that he could not meant only that whoever was observing him was keeping a good distance between them. He did not like it and he was going to tell Griz about it as soon as the big man came within range of the camp.

In the distance, Omaha caught the sound of Griz's old mule braying. Throwing a leg over Emily, he rode out to meet them, and did not give the camp a second thought. As yet there was nothing there to steal, and it was wide open. There would be nowhere for an intruder to hide himself as they approached. Omaha knew he might just be looking for trouble, but if anything broke, he knew it would be better for him and Griz to be together. It was possible that the probing eyes that Omaha felt belonged to another trapper or perhaps an Indian scouting for game, and he was merely a curiosity to whoever it was. A stranger to be observed at a distance, then left to go about his business, but Omaha did not believe that for one minute. It fit too closely with Cinnamon's arrival for him not to suspect it was somehow linked with her. Her wide-eyed apple-cheeked innocence did not do much for Omaha, though it seemed to do something for Grizzly. Something about her that Omaha could not quite put his finger on yet worried him, and he would be keeping an eye on her.

'Set up camp?' Griz called to him as Omaha approached on Emily, gingerly prancing sideways with pent-up energy.

'All we need is the grub and coffee,' Omaha said, then added to Griz in a low tone, 'I need to pass a few words with you.' He gave Cinnamon a solemn look that warned her the next words were not for her ears, and swung Emily away, putting their backs to her in a tight huddle.

'Trouble?' Griz asked in a gruff whisper.

'Not yet,' Omaha said softly, 'but there was someone near the camp watching me. Seemed like if he was after us it wouldn't do much good to find another place for the camp.'

Griz nodded. 'You're right. Where you figure this fella was?'

'North of the camp on high ground.'

'Might be lookin' for our new partner,' Griz mused to himself.

'That thought did cross my mind,' Omaha admitted.

'He'll have to go through me first.' Griz puffed out his chest, the heavy fur pelts that hung all over him rounding out until he looked like his namesake, the grizzly, unchallenged lord of the forest.

Omaha shrugged as if the entire matter did not really interest him. 'Let's go then.' Omaha raised his voice enough for Cinnamon to hear him clearly, then started Emily back toward the camp at a walk.

At the rate of speed the mule was content to travel, it took almost forty-five minutes for them to reach the campsite Omaha had begun to get ready. From the instant they arrived there, Ezra was nervous, slinking quickly from one side to another, coyote style, his pointed muzzle lifted up into the air sniffing wildly and making little half-barking, half-howling sounds that sent a shiver up Omaha's spine. There was something or had been someone there that Ezra did not like. Omaha knew something was wrong almost as quickly as the coyote. Nothing looked immediately different, but something had changed, and as Omaha piled out of Emily's saddle, looping the reins over the picket line, he saw it. A clear footprint was etched in a patch of bare earth where the pine needles had not collected near the picket line. Out of reflex at the footprint's close proximity to the line, Omaha glanced at the rope he had tied earlier. It was cut almost all the way through. It would no longer hold even a frantic mouse if the creature was determined to be free.

Griz unstrapped the wings from the mule's pack as he had taken to doing first thing, and propped them against a convenient tree trunk. Cinnamon pulled up beside Omaha and dismounted. As she reached to tie her scruffy mount on the picket line alongside Emily, Omaha opened his mouth to caution her about using a tree limb instead when the first shot split the air, coming from alarmingly nearby before he could get a word out. A second and a third followed closely on the heels of the first, and more followed, seeming to come in an explosive burst faster than a man could fire a gun. How many of them, he wondered, were out there?

His tail tucked between his legs, Ezra yelped and dove for the cover of the trees, sliding with a sideways list. Emily whinnied sharply and took off running with far from dainty speed. Cinnamon's horse jerked the reins from her hands and followed suit. Only Griz's old mule stood her ground, protesting loudly above the din raised by the gunshots and joined by Griz's hoarse yells. Luckily she was well protected by the huge tree trunks that ringed the clearing.

A sharp shove from Omaha sent Cinnamon to the ground sprawling on top of the thick carpet of pine needles. Omaha followed her down, winding up on top of her and jerking madly at the six-gun at his hip, where it had gotten hung up amongst the folds of Cinnamon's skirts. She squeaked and squirmed beneath him, giving Omaha ideas that should have been the furthest things from his mind in their situation.

Griz was on the ground bellowing like an enraged moose as the bullets flew around them like a swarm of vengeful wasps, snipping twigs off the branches above to fall in a gentle, erratic shower over them while others tugged at their clothes and whipped past within inches of their faces.

'Ohhhh,' Cinnamon whispered into Omaha's ear above her, 'don't let him take me back! He's a mean, cruel man, my uncle is.' The words spilled from her lips in a sudden flood, unmindful of the bullets that still snapped around them. 'I went to live with him a few years ago when my ma and pa were killed in a train wreck in the mountains outside Denver. He treats me like a slave, beats me when I do something he doesn't like. Don't let him take me back!' she pleaded, her small hands gripping the front of Omaha's shirt with surprising strength, her knuckles turning white with the strain. Full of tears, her large blue eyes stared up into his face.

Omaha was no hero. He had ended up on top of Cinnamon, and for the moment there was nowhere else for him to go. So he stayed, his flesh flinching at the thought of the bullet he might take for her at any moment, while another part of him was enjoying the soft feel of her beneath him, the warmth of her breath along his cheek as she poured out her story and plea for his protection.

At the moment to protect themselves meant protecting Cinnamon as well. Whoever was out there did not seem to want to ask questions or make demands. Omaha craned his neck around as the firing slowed and his eyes focused on the low burning embers of the fire he had started earlier, and just then another shot cracked through the air. Omaha blinked and looked again. Another bullet came whistling out of the fire. He swore under his breath in the language of the whites, finding words only there that fit the situation. Someone had thrown a handful of bullets into the fire and retreated before they started to go off to await the outcome. In another moment, Griz had climbed to his feet, his head swinging back and forth in search of their attacker like a big old grizzly looking for someone to send to his maker with a swipe of a paw.

Freeing his gun at last, Omaha started to rise as the gunshots faded out. Things quieted down and Cinnamon was again moving beneath Omaha, squirming to be free of his weight when it happened. Seemingly from out of nowhere a pair of battered boots appeared in front of Omaha's face, giving him about enough time to focus on them and hear Cinnamon's gasped exclamation of surprise before something whopped him across the side of the head with the force of a mule kick.

Omaha crumpled where he was, his fingers relaxing around his gun, not really unconscious, but dazed for a moment. Beneath his dead weight Cinnamon squirmed frantically, and then Omaha heard a string of whispered swearwords close to his ear such as he had not come across since he had spent some time in a bawdy house in a mining camp. Then a hand, large and rough-looking, appeared within the line of his blurred vision and grasped Cinnamon firmly about the wrist, dragging her from beneath Omaha in a very possessive manner.

At that point Omaha was not overly interested in Cinnamon's problems, but the stranger's assault on their camp was a different matter entirely. Under other circumstances Omaha might have just let the stranger take Cinnamon, as they obviously were well acquainted, but under other circumstances the bullets would not have been going off like a battleground, making it impossible for him to hear the man's approach and he would have been ready. As it was, he could not let the man take her, if only to prove a point. After all he did have his pride.

As Griz stormed in their direction Omaha

stuck out a hand, wrapping it firmly about the stranger's ankle, and gave it a good hard jerk.

Omaha's trick taking him completely by surprise, the stranger, broad in the shoulders and looking mean as a cross badger, flipped into the air like an upended jug and hit the ground like a felled tree. Cinnamon, still held in his viselike grip, sprawled on top of him and the two of them were bound together in a tangle of full skirts and flailing limbs. Cinnamon tried frantically to pull away while he tried to keep his grip on her.

Then, suddenly, Ezra burst into the clearing with a joyful yelp to intercept Griz, who was heading for the action with all the steam of a runaway locomotive. It took only an instant for the animal to realize that Griz was not going to stop, but even then it was already too late. All four legs braced out in different directions were not enough to bring Ezra up short of sliding directly into Griz's careening path. Griz, with eyes only for Cinnamon, the stranger, and Omaha sprawled on the ground before him, had not even taken note of Ezra's entrance onto the scene. Before he could realize what was happening, he stumbled over the coyote and was thrown into a headlong dive for the ground with no way to stop himself.

Omaha could actually feel the vibrations of the earth as Griz plowed into the ground and

71

saw the stranger, dark of hair and eye, disengage himself from Cinnamon with sudden determination, as if he had just made a hasty decision. Catlike, he was on his feet in an instant, running, legs pumping like pistons for the trees. Springing to his feet without a thought as to what he was going to do if he caught him, Omaha went after him.

'Wait!' Cinnamon yelled in a panic. 'He'll kill you!' were her only words of encouragement as Omaha disappeared into the fringe of trees in hot pursuit.

Regaining his feet, Griz set out after them both, leaving behind a disheveled Cinnamon, her mousy hair in tangles, her skirts scattered well above her knees, and a bewildered Ezra. Griz did not take the rifle, but instead snatched up the gun from where Omaha had dropped it and made tracks. Never a very fast runner, Griz could go distance with the best of them and he knew Omaha and the stranger could not be too far ahead. He could hear the pounding of running feet up ahead, and the long mournful howl of a bruised bedraggled coyote from behind.

Griz pressed on, his eyes automatically following the signs that lay on the ground before him. He was still running for all he was worth when Omaha appeared suddenly before him and he brought himself to a skidding halt. In the distance he could hear the pounding of hoofbeats rapidly fading.

'He got away,' Omaha said, gazing down a slope that dropped off like a cliff.

'How'd he get down there?' Griz asked curiously, breathing heavily from the run.

'Jumped,' Omaha replied, turning to head back for the camp as the shadows began to lengthen with the setting sun.

'Jumped?' Griz turned to follow, glancing back over his shoulder almost in awe.

'Jumped,' Omaha repeated with finality.

CHAPTER SIX

When Griz and Omaha made their way back to camp, Emily was already there waiting for them, putting her fine sleek nose out for a pat from Griz. The mule was still braying in the trees, but Cinnamon's scrubby horse was nowhere to be seen. The coyote, Ezra, insulted by his earlier treatment, accident or not, was sulking at Emily's side. Griz consoled him with an affectionate pat after he had secured the mule's tether to a stout young sapling.

'He's not going to give up this easy after what he tried,' Omaha commented as he gathered Emily's reins to mount up and go look for Cinnamon's horse. 'Her uncle's bound to try something again soon.'

Griz nodded absently, then turned a puzzled gaze on Omaha, 'Uncle?'

'She told me about her uncle and how mean he is to her when we were on the ground over there trying not to collect a stray bullet between us,' Omaha told him matter-of-factly, expecting Griz to know what he was talking about. 'You know,' Omaha persisted, seeing the strange look in Griz's eyes, 'about her folks getting killed and her uncle taking her in and treating her like a slave or something.'

Frowning, Griz shifted his gaze in Cinnamon's direction, where she was turning a flaming red from the roots of her hair to the tips of her booted toes.

'Told me she was kidnapped from a wagon train by Injuns, then sold by them to some fella who kept her up in these here mountains, beating her if she so much as said a word back to him.'

Together, Griz and Omaha turned to stare at Cinnamon, neither appearing too pleased with her.

Cinnamon shifted nervously on her feet, her shy glance going from one man to the other. From beneath lowered lashes that laid against her cheeks like soft moth's wings, she looked at the two men.

'I, I was afraid to tell you the truth,' Cinnamon stammered. 'Afraid if I did you wouldn't let me come with you, and I was afraid to be out here by myself.'

'You could have at least told us the same lie,' Omaha grumbled under his breath.

Tears brimmed in Cinnamon's eyes and she still did not meet the eyes of either of them. 'I'm sorry,' Cinnamon whispered. 'I'll tell you the truth now.' She sighed deeply, then started relaying the story with many pauses and stammerings.

'My parents did die several years ago,' Cinnamon began. 'There was no one to take care of me, so I had to take care of myself. I got mixed up with some people who were, well ... outlaws. I was only with them a few months, but word got out that I was with them, and now I've had this man after me so long I can hardly remember when it started.' Cinnamon's throat caught and she gave the appearance of being a little trapped bird attempting to flutter her way to freedom. 'I didn't *do* anything while I was with the Bunch,' she protested earnestly. 'They just took me in and looked after me. But that man is from the railroad, and he won't leave me alone. He says I was with the Bunch when they did their train robbing, and that makes me as guilty as them. You've got to believe me, I didn't *know* they were robbing trains, at least not right away, and I didn't have anywhere else to go anyway.'

'Just who was you with to make 'em want you that bad?' Griz asked, his curiosity not

75

letting him wait until Cinnamon got around to telling them outright.

'The railroad man calls them the Wild Bunch,' she answered in a soft, whispery voice, her eyes wide with innocence as if she had no idea of what she had just said.

Omaha and Griz exchanged long looks above Cinnamon's head. The Wild Bunch. Omaha did not think there was anyone left in that territory or any other one who did not know the name. The railroad was desperate to catch them. Could it be possible that Cinnamon had in fact gotten mixed up with the bunch of outlaws before the railroad had become so determined to track them down, and that now she was caught up in the manhunt that covered several states, territories, and even some foreign countries? Omaha doubted it.

It did not take Omaha long to round up Cinnamon's less than willing mount, but by the time he returned to camp, where Griz was keeping a tight watch, it was already after dark, and whatever work he could have gotten done on the wings with the skins Griz had provided, would have to wait for another time. And Omaha had decided for himself that as soon as they reached any kind of civilization, a town, or even a mining camp with some kind of transportation coming through, they were unloading Cinnamon. She would have to make it on her own from there.

The next couple of days went quickly, they making good time during the day, and camping early enough for Omaha to concentrate on the further repairs on his wings before sunset. Griz obligingly took the first watch each night and Omaha took the watch into the wee hours of the morning until they again took to the trail. After what had happened with whoever it was that was actually after Cinnamon, Griz and Omaha were not taking any chances on a surprise attack. Cinnamon was proving to be more help than Omaha had expected even though she did daydream a lot, often gazing off unseeingly into the distance.

Omaha ranged far ahead, scouting, looking for any sign of the character they had tangled with that night in camp, his efforts constantly rewarded by hoofprints, bootprints, and occasional remnants of fires ahead, or to the side of the trail they were following. Whoever the man was, he was sticking with them, and that in itself was more than enough to make Omaha nervous. Any man with that much determination had to be nothing but trouble.

For her part Emily, under Griz's instruction, was getting stronger and more powerfully winded every day. Omaha had let her run more than once, and when she cut loose it was like sitting a whirlwind. Griz had not exaggerated the horse's ability to run. She seemed to be born to it, tossing her head, pointing her nose into the wind and grabbing hastily for the bit each time Omaha turned her loose. There was no doubt in Omaha's mind that by the time they reached a town or mining camp, the horse would be able to take anything on four legs. If only he could be as sure about the progress of the repairs on his wings. Griz and Cinnamon had a way of using up his time, and he was also having some problems figuring out how to patch the wings properly so their ability to cup the wind and harness it would not be affected. Being so new at what he was doing, Omaha had to attack the problem slowly and with much thought or run the higher risk of failing badly even after he had already succeeded once. It occurred to him on several occasions that he should build a new pair of wings from scratch and junk the old ones that had gotten scarred in the tree, but that would take even more time than the method he was undertaking to use.

He was circling Emily back from a run to join up with Griz and Cinnamon when he spied them in earnest conversation with a stranger on foot. Omaha examined him as he hurried Emily in their direction. The stranger was ageless, square and thickset with curly blond hair and a thick beard of the same startling yellow color. Cinnamon sat

78

her horse in the background while Griz and the stranger exchanged words in an animated conversation that had broadcast itself to Omaha's ears in nothing so far but gibberish. The blond-haired stranger, Omaha discovered as he rode up, possessed blue eyes that were as startling as his blond hair. The man was gesturing wildly and speaking rapidly in a language he could not understand, interspersing a few words of English here and there that taken by themselves made no sense either. The look on the stranger's face, though, was one of concern, even pain.

Griz turned to Omaha as he rode up in a cloud of dust rising from beneath Emily's hurrying hoofs. 'I can't make nothing out of what he's sayin',' Griz complained. 'He talkin' in some Indian tongue?'

Omaha shook his head as he listened to the stranger go on with his torrent of words and wild gesticulating. Then, suddenly, it rang a bell far back in his mind.

'He's a Dutchman!' he said as if making a momentous discovery, remembering he had had occasion to hear German spoken back East when he had gone to school.

'You talk it?' Griz asked, looking more hopeful.

Omaha shook his head negatively, and listened more intently to the thickly accented, badly mauled English words the

79

blond-haired man was throwing in to spice up his tirade.

'Looks like he has some kind of trouble,' Cinnamon offered brightly when she could pull herself out of her own thoughts long enough to take note of what was happening. 'Maybe he wants you to help him.'

The stranger's eyes brightened when they lit on Cinnamon as she made her utterance and his head bobbed rapidly up and down. 'Ja, ja,' he repeated. 'Help.' He motioned for them to come with him and repeated the word in a heavy accent. 'Help.'

Griz needed no further urging. He started to go with the stranger, who had not even identified himself as far as they could tell from his babblings, but Omaha was inclined to be a little more cautious. Leaning out of the saddle he put a restraining hand on Griz's shoulder.

'Help what?' Omaha addressed the square, broad-shouldered stranger.

The stranger frowned a moment, then pointed to his own broad chest with a stubby finger. 'Otto,' he said seriously, 'help Otto.' He paused, gathering his resources, and gazed solemnly straight at Omaha. 'Little one,' he said, scraping his memory for meager bits of the language he had only just begun to learn. 'Little one coming.' He spread his hands helplessly. 'Trouble. I am,' he went on, frowning as he tried to pick out some words to get his message across, 'shoemaker. Don't know how to help...' He left the rest of the sentence unfinished and looked with pleading blue eyes from one to the other, searching for understanding.

Suddenly Cinnamon stared at him bug-eyed. 'He's talking about a baby!'

'Ja! Ja!' Otto exploded. 'A baby. Little one! Coming ... now.' He half turned away from them, gesturing with his whole body for them to come with him. 'Help Otto ... please.' The last word sounded more like a sneeze than a request for help.

Omaha shot Cinnamon an apprehensive sideways look. 'You know anything about birthing?'

'Are you kidding?' she exploded. 'If somebody cuts their finger I faint.'

Griz shrugged as Omaha turned his gaze on him. 'We can't know no less than he does,' he said quickly as he started to follow Otto. 'Besides, she might take kindly to having another woman close by right now.' Griz nodded meaningfully in Cinnamon's direction.

Cinnamon blanched and gave a little gulp, her fingers tightening on the reins she held. 'Me?'

Omaha reached out and gave Cinnamon's horse a light slap on the rump, sending it hustling along in Griz's wake as he followed Otto, the mule on a short lead. Otto led the

81

way into a grove of aspen, their leaves and branches stirring on the mountain breeze, their leaves shimmering like freshly minted silver dollars. The distance they covered was short, Otto having apparently spotted them from his camp and run after them to plead for help. Omaha was not sure what he could do to help, but he had been around during a couple of bad birthings with animals.

The four of them, with horses and mules, hit the small clearing in the trees like a stampede, and when Omaha glanced around for some sign of a woman moaning in pain and near her time, he saw only a pine pallet and sprawled across it, a horse. No one else was around. Omaha was beginning to have doubts about Otto's sanity until he gave the horse a closer look. The animal was suffering intensely, sides heaving, belly still distended with the foal she was struggling to give birth to.

Cinnamon almost fell out of the saddle with relief, rushing to Otto's side where he was stroking the horse's sweat-streaked neck and whispering soft, foreign encouragements in her ear. It was plain to even Cinnamon's meager knowledge that something was wrong and the mare was in a bad way.

'Poor thing,' Cinnamon crooned, then half turned to Omaha where he had dismounted and joined them beside the animal. 'Is she going to die?'

Otto's head jerked around at the sound of Cinnamon's last word. 'Nein. No!' he said firmly. 'Not die!'

The mare did not appear to be anything special, but Omaha could understand his concern as he knelt beside the straining animal. She was no beauty like Emily, but if she died, Otto would be alone on foot in what was a very hostile land. Omaha did not know how far it was to the mining camp they had struck out for, but he had seen no sign of it yet when scouting ahead. By that measure alone it would be more than a short hike.

Griz leaned over Omaha's shoulder as he checked to see what the mare's trouble was. Omaha was learning firsthand and fast that Griz had an unnerving habit of volunteering for things he knew nothing about. He made no move to get down on the ground beside him and give him a hand, but stayed where he was behind Omaha half bent over, his large hands braced on his knees.

'You got any idea what's ailing her?' Griz asked, his voice filled with sympathy, his thoughts undoubtedly going to his own Emily.

Omaha nodded. 'Breech birth,' he said with authority despite the fact he had only seen it once before and then had had no hand in correcting the situation. 'The foal is backwards,' he said in further explanation. 'We have to turn it around.'

'Inside?' Griz asked, and Omaha thought he could detect a slight green tinge to his pallor.

'If we don't,' Omaha returned, 'they'll both die.'

Griz paused, the somber look still in place on his face. 'Well, go ahead, boy,' he said at last, throwing it in Omaha's lap, 'you do what you have to and we'll hold her down.'

Omaha doubted that the mare, already having spent long hours in labor, would need much holding down; she was getting weaker by the minute. But the job he was about to tackle was essentially a one-man undertaking, and he was the only one there who had so much as seen what had to be done. For the horse's sake, there was no time for them to be debating over who was going to lend a hand. With a sigh, Omaha leaned into the job. It would have been much easier if it had been a baby person as Cinnamon had first assumed instead of a baby horse.

Even as he bent to his task the one question foremost in Omaha's mind had to do with what a Dutchman, almost non-English-speaking immigrant shoemaker, was doing in the middle of nowhere with a pregnant horse. It did not seem like a course a wise man might follow.

At the head, Otto continued to murmur soft assurances to the panicked, wild-eyed beast, none of it understandable to anyone but the horse, and at the tail Omaha was attempting to do what he had seen done only once before.

At first the mare did not seem to mind, but when Omaha started pushing the foal back the way it had come, she took exception to the situation. Swinging a leg forcefully back, she somehow managed to catch Omaha across the shin with a blow that took him totally by surprise and completely dispelled the myth of the stoic Indian who never yelled out in pain.

Omaha bellowed like a bull buffalo, then started swearing in Griz's direction just before the mare he thought completely exhausted kicked him again, sending him rolling like a popped wine cork across a table of pine boughs and aspen leaves.

As he came to his knees in the leaves he swore with even greater gusto, and becoming aware of one shin and one hip throbbing with the force of the mare's kicks, Omaha moaned, more for the fact that he was going to have to start again from the beginning than from the pain he suddenly found himself in.

'You said you were going to hold her!' he bellowed at Griz, the sting of the kicks still traveling up his leg like a shock.

'Did,' Griz grunted in a querulous tone, 'just didn't hold the right part of her. Didn't know she was plannin' on kickin' you.'

'Well, now you know,' Omaha snapped, dragging himself back to the mare's side.

Cinnamon knelt beside the mare's head with the Dutchman alternately stroking the animal's sleek head, and clasping and unclasping her hands nervously. Never in her young life had she witnessed the birthing of anything, except a baby chick hatching out of an egg, but you could not count that.

'Maybe,' she suggested timidly above Omaha's almost unbroken stream of swearing, 'maybe we should let her take care of this herself.'

'Can't,' Omaha said with hardly a sideways glance. 'Told you before, it's already been too long. She needs help. That foal won't turn itself around.'

Without comment, the Dutchman grabbed Cinnamon's hand, pulling her back to soothing the frightened creature, and motioned Omaha to get on with what he was doing. Cinnamon, patting the horse and talking quietly to it, could not help glancing continually over her shoulder to see what Omaha was doing.

Griz had hold of the mare's back legs now, putting himself between the hoofs and Omaha, the heavy fur of his pelts cushioning him against the kicks she insisted on delivering now with regularity.

With new determination Omaha went about his task, and was startled by the almost instant progress he made with his second start. He could feel the small creature within against his hand as he pushed it once again back the way it had come. It occurred to Omaha that by now the little fellow must be beginning to feel as if he was not wanted at all. Omaha shifted position, then, suddenly, manipulating the foal with one hand, he was turning it. Sweat was pouring off him, but Omaha was grinning. It was going to work. A bit further and he felt the sharp little hoofs, then the tiny velvet muzzle. Then it was as if the mare suddenly realized the problem had been solved and she took up her chore in earnest, the pressure almost strangling Omaha's arm as he struggled to keep his hold on the foal as it started for the third time back toward daylight. Not liking his powerful grip on her legs the horse gave Griz a couple more good kicks, but Griz hung on and Omaha brought the new foal steadily forward within his grip until the nose and forelegs appeared, followed rapidly by the rest of the tiny, skinny body, and the ordeal was at an end.

For the moment the mother was in no condition to help, so Omaha cleared the tiny nostrils after cutting the cord, then grabbed up handfuls of pine needles and started rubbing the colt's body briskly, cleaning him off and getting him to take notice.

The new arrival did not need much urging

87

to do that. Almost from the moment Omaha had begun to rub him, the little fellow's head had come up, peering around him as if in awed surprise. After a short time had passed, the new colt gave a miniature snort and began struggling in Omaha's grasp, trying to rise. Omaha let him try it and a moment later the small creature was sprawled out in the pine needles again, his sides heaving from the effort, as he immediately gathered himself to try again.

Otto beamed as he saw the mare roll up, gather her legs beneath her and then stagger up. She swayed unsteadily on her feet, but remained standing. The same could not be said for her new son, who managed to position his spindly legs beneath him well enough to gain his feet, then spilled into the needles a second time, almost bouncing back for a third try. Finally he managed to get all four legs under control enough to stand there spraddle-legged, in unsteady triumph. Otto was exclaiming jubilantly in the language none of them understood, and stroking the mare's neck enthusiastically.

Cinnamon threw her arms around Omaha's neck. 'You did it, Omaha! You did it!' Releasing him, she turned again to gaze at the unsteady newcomer with the large, flared nostrils and enormous eyes that were twin pools of intelligence set in a delicate dish-shaped face accented by a blaze that almost looked like striking lightning. 'He's beautiful,' she breathed.

'You make a damn fine midwife,' Griz exclaimed by way of congratulation. 'Have to make sure you're somewheres around if my Emily ever needs one.'

CHAPTER SEVEN

Griz used the time, place, and circumstances as a reason to stop for the day, as well as an excuse to stay over the next day. He cited the undeniable fact that they were in need of meat and that he had had little success hunting on the trail with Cinnamon chattering in his ear most of the time and the mule acting up because of Omaha's wings strapped to her back.

Barely picking himself up off the ground, plastered from head to toe in filth and exhausted to the marrow of his bones, Omaha voiced no objections to the announcement when Griz made it. In fact, it would finally give him some uninterrupted time to work on his wings.

To Griz's way of thinking, Omaha had to have his brains scrambled where his obsession with flying was concerned. It crossed his mind to wonder if maybe he had been out in the hot sun without a hat too long at some point along the way. Possibly his obsession was somehow related to his background. In Griz's experience, half-breeds had always been a strange lot. Not that he was a man to say anything against mixed blood, or for it for that matter, but some of the odd personality quirks he had come across seemed to be peculiar to them. Especially obsessions. Seemed like every one he had ever known had had some driving force behind him, something always eating at him.

Shaking his head, Griz gathered up his rifle and shells while he watched Omaha carefully untie the unwieldy wings from the mule's pack. At the other side of the camp Griz could see Otto watching intently, a curious expression on his face. That was what Griz had been hoping for when he had announced that they would stay there a spell. The Dutchman was a shoemaker. And to Griz that meant he knew how to work with hides, and it was just possible he might be able to give Omaha a hand. Just because Griz figured there were times when Omaha was not playing with a full deck, was no reason for him not to want to see that Omaha got what he was after. After all, they did have a partnership. And even though Griz figured that riding Emily should be the closest any man ever got to flying, he was not small enough to deny Omaha any chance that might come along.

As Omaha carried the wings to near where the fire burned, Cinnamon appeared as if out of nowhere. When he seated himself a short distance from the fire, she followed suit, sitting very close to him, her legs crossed Indian style, her skirts tucked in around her knees. Although she had seen the wings before, she had never really looked at them close up. Now, as she stared at them, she became aware of the thick leather thongs that had bound Omaha's arms to the wings, cut through with a sharp blade, and she frowned.

'How do you get out of them?' she asked innocently, her blue eyes wide and sparkling.

'He don't,' Griz said with a dry chuckle as he passed them headed out of camp. 'He gets himself caught in trees and waits for folks like me to climb up and cut him down.' With a parting chuckle, Griz left camp, Ezra on his heels.

Cinnamon looked thoroughly shocked. 'You mean there's no way for you to get out once you're tied in?'

Omaha shrugged. It had not seemed that important a detail when he had started out. The crash landing in the tree had told him something, but as yet he had come up with no ideas on how to remedy the problem.

'It's not important,' Omaha blustered. 'First, I have to fly, then the rest will come,' he told her, not willing to let Cinnamon see his uncertainty.

Frowning a moment Cinnamon paused, then brightened. 'Why don't you just put a handgrip near the end of each wing, and only tie your arm in above the elbows?' She held her arms out like a scarecrow, letting them drop from the elbows, showing how easy it would be to reach either side of his body with the forearm free. 'Then have the rawhide tied so you can reach the end of it hanging down by your side, where you can untie it just by pulling the end.'

There followed Cinnamon's suggestion a moment when Omaha stared at her hardly able to believe what she had just said, and the simplicity of the answer to his problem. There still remained the problem of how to tie the thongs so they could be easily pulled free by the dangling strip and yet not untie by themselves when he was airborne, but Omaha knew Cinnamon had given him the answer. That, though, was still one of his least important problems. He had barely begun to make repairs on the rips and holes in the surface of the wings themselves. A lot more work had to be done before he would be ready to fly again.

Otto, as it turned out, understood more of the new language he was learning than he spoke. And it did not take much understanding of language for him to see the odd contraption Omaha had, and his intention to repair it with the large strips of well-tanned leather he had laid out beside him.

Neither Omaha nor Cinnamon noticed Otto disappear from their midst. Moments later he reappeared, his arms laden with a pot of glue, sharp blade for trimming, package of needles, spools of fine gut for sewing, and a brush for the glue. Dropping down beside Omaha, he carefully arranged his supplies, then grinned at him.

'I shoemaker, ja,' he said haltingly. 'Now ... I help you.' He grinned, picking up Omaha's leather to gaze at it, then the leather already on the wings with a critical eye. After a minute or two of inspection his head bobbed up and down in enthusiastic approval. 'Ja, ja,' he muttered under his breath, then began the work with an efficiency that bordered on wizardry.

Deftly, Otto applied glue to a trimmed piece of leather, then placed it over the hole it had been cut to fit. Following that he sewed the edges down with tiny stitches that almost welded one piece of leather to the other, then coated the whole surface with another coat of glue, completely sealing it. Both Omaha and Cinnamon, using gut and needles Otto had provided, worked laboriously over one hole, each trying to emulate his actions using tiny stitches and following Otto's quick, sure movements with envious glances.

By the time Griz returned to camp, fresh meat wrapped in the new pelt he had to add to his collection, the work Omaha had estimated to take many days or even weeks of his time was all but complete. Otto slaved over the wings as if it was a labor of love until it was too dark to see. Early the next morning, when the light of dawn was barely lighting the camp, he was at it again, finishing up the last few rips before the sun had even cleared the mountaintops. Then with sign language and the persistent repeating of what he wanted, Omaha managed to get across to Otto what was needed on the underside of the wings for his supports, the handgrips, and the special ties. Cinnamon's ideas. The rest of the day was spent on making the adjustments and by sunset, Omaha was ready to fly again.

'When are you going to test it?' Cinnamon asked eagerly.

'Not soon,' Griz grumbled. 'He can't go getting himself busted up 'til he rides some races for me. We got us a partnership.'

Cinnamon gazed at the wings dreamy-eyed. 'Will you take me flying with you sometime, Omaha?'

Omaha shook his head. 'It's not safe.'

'But you did it,' Cinnamon protested. 'You did it and it worked. I saw you. It looked like heaven.'

'It's not the kind of thing a woman should get involved with,' Omaha persisted. 'People would think you were loony. Make it hard for you to get married.'

'Ain't nothin' could make it hard for a woman to get married in these parts,' Griz interjected.

Omaha glared at him. 'I'm testing the wings tomorrow when we break camp,' he said suddenly.

'How?' Griz demanded. 'There ain't no cliff for you to jump off around here.'

'I'll test them,' Omaha said with set jaw. 'All I need is Emily and Cinnamon's help.'

'I'll help,' Cinnamon said eagerly.

Griz sighed. 'Damn fool half-breed!' he muttered under his breath. 'You can use Emily, long as it ain't nothin' can hurt her,' he conceded, rolling into his blankets.

Cinnamon's creamy skin was flushed with the excitement of the coming day. Omaha leaned back against Emily's saddle gazing up toward the stars that lit the night sky like burning embers, and was content.

The next day dawned in perfect flying weather. The sky was a brilliant blue marked by only an occasional cloud that hurried along on the brisk breezes of the higher altitudes. Treetops bent before the gentle breeze that swept down out of the mountains looming to the north of them. The huge mountains that Griz lovingly called Ol' Red almost glowed in the bright splash of morning light, with splotches of snow standing out in stark white contrast to the rusty red of the mountains' hulk. Omaha breathed in the crisp morning air like a tonic as Cinnamon and the Dutchman tied the thongs along the bottom of the wings in the new way Cinnamon had devised. It was the second tying. The first time Cinnamon had insisted he untie the dangling strings with his fingertips after freeing his hands from the new grips to make sure everything was working the way they had planned. It had. Now he was going to fly again. Omaha could feel it in his bones.

Omaha had given Cinnamon her instructions carefully, and more than once, to be sure she understood what was expected of her when she was up on Emily with one end of the rope looped around the saddle horn and the other attached to Omaha and his precious wings. The rope was looped carefully around the framework of the wings that centered around Omaha's body and rigged so he could pull it loose once he was airborne, something he would not have been able to do before they had come up with the idea of handgrips near the ends of the wings instead of thongs the whole length. Although Omaha was glad of Cinnamon's helpful suggestions, he hoped she was not depending on too much in the way of gratitude.

His wings tied again in place, Omaha sucked the cool air into his lungs, feeling them expand, while Cinnamon moved to Emily's side and stepped gracefully up into the leather. She knew exactly what she was to do. They had gone over it often, and if all went well, timing would be important. She was to start Emily out slowly, letting Omaha trot along behind, getting the feel of it, then gradually increase the horse's speed. At that point Omaha would have to be running, still attached to the clumsy wings, but he had seen plenty of birds that had not looked exactly graceful on the ground, but commanded the sky when they took to the air. His own plans were simple and along similar lines. Once he was running, and Emily pulling, the movement of the air itself, the breeze would have an uplifting effect on the wings and he would be able to lift his legs clear of the ground. It was at that instant that Cinnamon was to give Emily her head, line her out at a dead run, and Omaha had no doubt that he would take to the air like an eagle. It was all in the timing. Once he was indeed airborne behind Emily, he would be able to jerk the rope free and glide on his own.

Muttering to himself in a querulous tone, Griz stood back from the others, holding the mule's lead rope, while staring in mute disbelief at the scene unfolding before him. Even Otto had gotten himself caught up in the situation as if he actually expected the contraption to work. Maybe it had worked that one time before, but Griz was convinced that it had been nothing but dumb luck, and he was not even sure if it had been good or bad luck that had swept Omaha along on the wind. It had fed his obsession and Griz knew the last thing a man like Omaha Jones needed was encouragement. One of these times he was bound to break his fool neck, and Griz hoped it would not be until after he had ridden the races for the season up on Emily's back. He had seen the way Omaha sat her, the way they moved together, and knew something good when he saw it. Omaha was without a doubt the best rider he had ever had sitting on Emily's back. He was a compact man, and he rode like he was a part of the horse himself. Besides, Griz hated to think of trying to locate another rider with their first stop only a couple of days away. He gave Otto a sideways speculative glance and shook his head slightly. The Dutchman just did not fit. He was too blocky. And, while the vision of the Dutchman up on Emily's back would make the townspeople as well as the miners bet more heavily against her, the catch would be that Griz could not be sure of the little horse's ability to win with that much weight on her back. Besides, as Otto continually pointed out in his stilted English, he was a shoemaker.

Cinnamon gave one last glance over her shoulder for Omaha's okay before she touched her heel to Emily's side, starting her forward. The rope between her and Omaha to the rear went suddenly taut as Omaha let the slack be taken up between them when Emily started out. Cinnamon raised Emily to an even trot, and Omaha came along behind at the end of the rope, feeling the surge of the air beneath his wings. Exhilaration coursed through his taut body like electricity as he increased the tempo of his pumping legs to keep up with Emily's increased speed.

Continually, Cinnamon glanced back over her shoulder, watching for signs of trouble, apprehensive that Omaha would end up face down on the ground, being dragged along at the end of the rope Emily trailed. But somehow he kept up, even as Emily lengthened her strides. And every few strides that Omaha took, Cinnamon could see him jump into the air, wings tipped to the sky. His hops were ended by a short glide back to the ground and a resumption of his uneven run. Again and again he hopped, reaching for the clouds. Griz and Otto stood by, watching in fascination as Cinnamon and Omaha drew further and further away, hopscotching it across the long valley.

Omaha was up and down so many times it almost made Griz's neck ache from watching.

Omaha could feel the burning in his lungs as he sucked the air inside like a flood and felt the warmth of his own blood pumping like surging rivers through his veins. Jumping again, he felt the lift of the wind against his wings, but he did not glide more than a few feet before he was again careening along behind Emily at a stumbling run. It was there. He could feel it. The strange pull of the wind, the lifting sensation that he had felt before when he had stepped off into space from the peak of El Capitan. But, for some reason, he just could not catch the wind. Each time he thought he had it, it would dump him unceremoniously back to the grass-covered valley floor. Somehow Omaha had managed to keep from falling, and each time his feet touched the ground he felt as if they were just skimming over the top of the grasses, as if his strides were getting longer. Eyes bulging with exertion Omaha stared ahead and saw the once distant stand of trees looming closer like an unscalable castle wall. The length of the valley was fast running out. Omaha realized he should be signaling Cinnamon to stop so he could rest, then try again from the far end of the valley, but that was one thing they had forgotten to work out between them. They had no signal to indicate he wanted to stop, and his pride would not permit him to bellow for her to stop when this whole thing had been his idea. All that was left was to stumble along behind until she got close to the trees and pulled Emily up of her own accord.

Resigning himself to the completion of the punishing run, Omaha gritted his teeth and pounded on. What Omaha had no way of knowing was that his strides *were* getting longer. He was running like a deer through the rippling grasses, and the pull of the rope before him was putting more and more space between the place where one foot left the ground and the other again touched down. He ran on like that, in something less than graceful bounds, until, suddenly, the wind shifted, and he found himself headed directly into it. For long seconds, he was appalled at the effort it took to head into the wind. His legs felt like lead, and the pounding of the blood through his veins felt as if it would surely make them burst.

Then, as suddenly as the wind changed, there came a lift that felt as if a giant hand had plucked him from the ground and into the sky. In an instant he was gliding on the wind, only dimly aware of the fact that Cinnamon was following his instructions and had put Emily into a hard run. The increased speed gave Omaha some additional height, but even in his mood of dizzy exultation, he could see that it was not enough. Without thinking, Cinnamon was heading Emily for a hole in the trees. Caught up in the excitement of Omaha's success, she did not realize he would not be able to clear the trees, and even if he did, the rope would be tangled in the spreading limbs before she had penetrated the thick stand of aspen more than a few feet. Omaha hated to give up his brief tryst with the wind, but there seemed to be no other choice. He could not risk his wings being mangled again.

Knowing he had not enough height to glide long on his own, Omaha freed one hand from the wing's grip and jerked his end of the rope free. Feeling the slack in her end of the rope almost instantly, Cinnamon pulled Emily up sharply and turned in the saddle expecting to see Omaha soaring free as he had the first time when he had passed overhead, and she had spotted him by sheer accident.

Instead, Cinnamon, Griz, and Otto watched with mouths agape as Omaha careened into a one-hundred-and-eighty-degree turn, one wing tip extended toward the ground, and he spun full around like a top. The soaring heights Cinnamon had expected were nowhere in evidence as Omaha slid sideways on the wind, headed for the ground like a wounded duck. It all happened so fast Cinnamon could hardly believe she had been a witness to it at all. One moment Omaha was flying, the next he slid into a belly-crash landing that made her cringe where she sat the saddle while both Griz and Otto ran like madmen to where Omaha lay beneath his wings, inert. Wheeling Emily, Cinnamon rushed to join them.

As they approached they could see the wings tipping slowly from side to side as Omaha attempted to gather himself enough to free a hand from one of the grips and jerk the leather thongs free. In the end it was Griz who did it for him, dragging his limp form from beneath the ill-fated wings.

'Anything broke?' Griz asked anxiously.

'Don't think so,' Omaha replied through a haze. 'I didn't hear any of the wood splinter when I hit. It didn't get any new rips, did it?'

With a grunt of disgust, Griz dropped Omaha back onto the grass, where he sprawled for a moment like a limp rag doll before getting his breath back enough to roll to his knees.

'What I need,' he began through gasping breaths, 'is another place to jump off of. It must be the height,' he mused as Cinnamon slid off Emily's back and came running to drop herself in the grass beside Omaha, reaching out to pull him against herself, cradling his head against her bosom.

'Are you all right?' she breathed anxiously

in his ear. 'I thought for sure you got yourself killed when I saw you fall.'

Relaxing against the softness of her grasp, Omaha let his thoughts wander when, suddenly, above the sound of her rapid heartbeat against his ear, he became aware of the distant sound of rushing water for the first time. The sound was familiar to him. It was made when water was flowing down through a gorge. Omaha stayed where he was, enjoying the sensation of Cinnamon being so close to him, catching his breath, and smiled.

CHAPTER EIGHT

Once Omaha had regained his breath and ascertained that no new damage had been inflicted on the wings, he was eager to press on. The damage to himself in the fall had been minimal, a few bruises across his broad bronze chest and a few scrapes the lengths of his arms. It had been worth it though, to catch the wind for even a few seconds.

The distant roar of the plunging river got louder and clearer after Omaha had regained his senses, and they were journeying toward it. He had said nothing about what he was planning if there was indeed a gorge along with the river up ahead, knowing Griz would be dead set against it. There would be time enough to argue that out when they reached the river, and by the ever increasing din, Omaha knew that would be very soon.

Cinnamon had been unusually silent since Omaha's fall, and he noticed the fact even if he did not know the reason for it. She rode beside him, often casting sidelong glances his way that were a puzzle to him. He never had been able to figure out women, so as the wind blew in their faces Omaha pondered Cinnamon where she rode beside him, her hair ruffled by the stiff breeze, a high flush whipped into her white cheeks, and her skirts blowing so that many were the times when Omaha got a glimpse of leg all the way up to her knee. Cinnamon did not seem to be aware of the display. For a time longer they rode on like that, Griz and Otto bringing up the rear conversing in half sentences and sign language, and Cinnamon not saying anything at all until Omaha was ready to break free to scout ahead. Then, suddenly, she spoke.

'Was it my fault that you fell?' she asked Omaha concernedly. 'Did I do something?'

'No,' Omaha lied quickly, knowing it was at least in part her fault, though in such a new thing as flying it would always be difficult to place blame anywhere. What had happened had happened. He would simply have to try again.

'Are you sure?' Cinnamon persisted, gazing at him from beneath lowered lashes.

Almost without their noticing it the roar of the water was growing steadily louder, and Omaha had to raise his voice to reassure Cinnamon and be heard. 'I'm sure,' he said loudly, then urged Emily on ahead to scout the area. He was acutely aware of the fact that whoever was after Cinnamon was still out there, ranging well ahead of them. More often than not he had picked up signs, though he had made no mention of it to Cinnamon.

If there was indeed a gorge up ahead, it could be a good place for an ambush by almost anyone. Outlaws after their horses and supplies, unfriendly Indians, though Omaha was not familiar with what tribes would frequent that area. And then, of course, there was the determined soul who still stuck close to where Cinnamon was. As yet they had not had any more trouble with him, but Omaha had a feeling deep in his bones that they would.

Wrapped in his thoughts as he approached the source of the roaring sound of rushing water, Omaha was aware only of the rhythmic beat of Emily's hoofs beneath him and what sign he could spot. It took him many minutes of being aware of, but not really acknowledging the beat of hoofs coming up behind him, the gait of

Cinnamon's mount. He had heard it, been aware of it, but it had posed no threat and his conscious mind had chosen to ignore it until Cinnamon was almost upon him.

When Omaha turned, it was to tear his attention from the river far below, the source of the rushing sound that had drawn him. It was not like the Goosenecks, a plunging gorge with high walls on either side of the river. It was instead bordered on one side by a high and steep rise where he sat, Emily gazing down, and on the other by a long grassy bench that led into another thick stand of aspen. Pine showed itself on a slope some distance behind the trees that shimmered near the river's bank. The water below was moving with exceptional swiftness and the roar hung on the air with a fine mist as the water poured out of the rapids just north of them flowing into smooth water below. There had to be a trail leading down to a ford. But Omaha had not yet had time to scout it, and he was sure Griz would know it, traveling the same route as he did each year.

'Oh my,' Cinnamon said quietly as she pulled her horse up beside Omaha, her voice almost inaudible above the river's roar. 'How are we going to get down?'

'Griz knows the way,' Omaha said offhandedly, but what he was really thinking about was the wind in his face. The blowing of the wind, the way it rippled through the trees far below.

There was something about the wind blowing against him that Omaha was beginning to associate with flight. It seemed as if each time he took to the air the wind was blowing against him. It was then that he got the most lift. He wondered about it. When Griz arrived with the mule and his wings, he would find out. The circumstances were not perfect with the thick stand of trees on the far side of the broad river to snag him, but they probably would not come across a better spot for many a mile.

Omaha's gray eyes swept the distant bank again, and for an instant, something caught and held his attention. Something had moved quite a distance south of them on the river's far side. A shadow within a shadow had appeared for a moment. Though the sun was glowing brightly and Omaha concentrated on the spot, he could not see the thing again. He shrugged unconsciously. It had probably been his imagination.

'What are you looking at?' Cinnamon broke into his thoughts, gazing without blinking in the same direction as he.

'Just seeing if I can land over there all right.'

'You're going to try it again ... here?' Cinnamon asked almost in awe of his determination.

Omaha nodded. 'Just as soon as Griz brings up my wings.'

Cinnamon stared down at the swirling blue waters below. 'I can't swim,' she announced.

'You don't have to swim,' Omaha countered. 'Just hang on to your horse and let him swim.'

'Fly me over,' Cinnamon begged. 'It's not very far, and I don't weigh much.'

'No,' Omaha told her firmly as Griz and Otto finally came ambling up.

'I can't swim,' Cinnamon repeated to everyone at large.

'Ain't too deep,' Griz commented, forgetting that he had long ago measured the depth against himself and Cinnamon was much smaller. 'Just hold onto the saddle horn and your hoss'll take you across just fine.'

Cinnamon bit her lip and shook her head worriedly as Omaha got to untying the wings from the mule's back. 'I can't swim,' she repeated in a more insistent tone.

'What the hell *you* doin' now!' Griz demanded in a bellow, catching sight of Omaha maneuvering the awkward wings.

'I'm going to cross this way,' Omaha announced calmly as he began wrestling with the fastenings, Cinnamon helping him in spite of her pout. 'I should be able to land easily on that bench across the river,' he told

Griz, not at all sure where he would end up once he stepped off into space.

Otto's eyes twinkled in anticipation, but Griz as usual thrust his lantern jaw out in anger. 'Are you plum loco?' Griz shouted at him. 'You already near kilt yourself once today. Reckon you got to try it again, do you? Don't know why I ever wanted the shoemaker here to help you fix them damn things. We was a lot better off before. We're partners, you an' me,' Griz persisted. 'Now, how you gonna do your part if you go and get yourself all busted up before we even *see* a town?'

'I'll do my part,' Omaha assured him. 'The rest of you just take the trail down to the bank and I'll cross as soon as I see you're down all right. I'll meet you on the other side.'

Griz grunted irritably, but there was no help for it. In his own way, he had found Omaha to be every bit as stubborn as he was himself. There would be no dissuading him from what he was about. Picking up Emily's reins along with the mule's lead, Griz led the way toward the trail that cut its way down the face of the rock rise. The coyote, Ezra, trotted on ahead while Cinnamon and Otto brought up the rear, Cinnamon looking a bit pale and nervous.

The trail, while steep, and rough in places, was an easy one to negotiate, especially when folks had enough good sense to climb down off their horses and lead them down. When he looked back over his shoulder, Griz could see Omaha standing on the edge of the drop-off where they had left him.

It was instantly apparent that Omaha had spied them at the base of the trail as his form seemed to hesitate a moment at the edge of the bluff, then launch itself out into open air.

Cinnamon gasped. Otto was spellbound. Griz swore.

Suspended on air for a moment as if he could not go backwards or forwards, Omaha was aware of the three upturned faces below watching him with intent concentration. Then, as if breaking the grip of what held him, Omaha swooped forward in a daring dive toward the river's surface. He gathered momentum going down, then stalled as a blast of wind slammed into him, sending him into a glide that almost skimmed the surface of the surging water. Somehow, above the exhilaration of the flight, Omaha managed to remember to extend his legs, birdlike, as he approached the riverbank with a speed that whipped tears into his eyes and blurred the green grass as it swept up to meet him. He felt the hard earth under his feet as the impetus of the wind continued to carry him forward in large running leaps in an effort to keep from being knocked headlong to the ground.

Omaha hit the soft muddy bank on his knees and thought that was where it would end, but life is never simple. The wind that had carried him billowed beneath the wings as he jerked to an abrupt halt on his knees, then, as Omaha released his handgrips, reaching quickly for the leather thongs that dangled at his sides, he felt the irresistible surge of the wind as it snagged him like a tumbleweed, tumbling him over in a somersault that left him sprawled on his back, the wings flat beneath him. Luckily, the wings flat along the ground, the wind could catch them no more and Omaha let his breath out in a long sigh. Again reaching for the thongs that bound him he heard a high-pitched shriek of panic that made his fingers fumble as he craned his head around enough to see the river over his shoulder. The now familiar words followed in a long wail.

'I can't swim!' Cinnamon gurgled as she floundered helplessly in the grips of the river's swift current, and was swept away with startling speed.

Jerking the leather cords free, Omaha jumped to his feet. Griz was almost on top of him, having entered the river first, Ezra perched on top of the mule's pack. He had to have been better than halfway across when Cinnamon had started after him astride her stolen pony, and Otto, his arms full of colt,

112

had apparently started across behind her before the disaster had struck.

Weighted down by heavy pelts attached to him at every quarter, and holding two animals on lead, Griz was helpless to do anything at the instant that Cinnamon had left the saddle but bellow.

'It's not deep!' Griz roared across the ever widening distance between them. 'Get your feet under you!'

The current, though, was far too swift for that, and Cinnamon continued to flounder helplessly while the river carried her farther and farther downstream as she bobbed and ducked in the water spluttering and shrieking the whole time, her cries getting fainter, lost in the roar of the wild river.

'Omaha!' was the last word discernible to anybody as Griz came out of the water dripping and staggering beneath his own sodden weight. Not being a bear in actual fact, he could not even shake himself to rid the many pelts he wore of the heavy moisture that clung to them.

Hurrying his horse forward, Otto herded Cinnamon's abandoned mount out of the river, staring at Griz and Omaha with open-mouthed concern, his face an almost pasty white as Omaha snatched Emily's reins from Griz's hands and hit the saddle in a flying mount as he put her to a run before he was even half in the saddle. Ahead, he could barely see Cinnamon still floundering in the river's grip.

'I also cannot swim,' Omaha heard Otto confessing to Griz as he tore off downstream.

There was no way for Omaha to know exactly what had happened to Cinnamon, he could only speculate. The pony had probably hit a deep spot where it had been forced to swim for a few strides and during that short time something had spooked him. From Cinnamon's attitude earlier, Omaha was almost equally sure it had to have been she who did it. But, whatever the reasons, there was no question that she needed help now.

Emily was running full out, her hoofs making soft sucking sounds in the mucky earth that bordered the meandering river, and Omaha was gaining on Cinnamon with every stride. Somehow, in spite of her claims of not being able to swim, she was keeping her head above water more than it was under. And, up ahead, the current seemed to slow. Leaning low over Emily's neck, Omaha let her out, urging her to speeds he had never thought of before with the game horse. Emily responded eagerly as she stretched her neck out, leaning into the bit, her ears flicking constantly toward the rear to pick up Omaha's words of encouragement.

Omaha was coming on strong, Cinnamon's last cry ringing in his ears, when he saw the other rider appear from the shelter of the trees ahead of Cinnamon's path, and send his horse into the water to intercept her. Omaha felt he should be drawing a breath of relief, but his view of Cinnamon, now clear to his sight, told him differently. She was suddenly throwing herself sideways in the water, snatching at it, splashing up vast sprays of the river's muddy waters in an effort to pull herself away from the ominous rider who bore down on her with relentless ease from the riverbank ahead.

The stranger kneed his horse around in front of Cinnamon and plucked her from the river's icy grip with ease, ignominiously depositing her over the front of his saddle before heading back for the riverbank. Omaha barely had time to catch a glimpse of Cinnamon's lithe form, her soaked clothes clinging to her every curve, before she disappeared into the trees in the stranger's possessive grip.

Dumbfounded by what had just happened, Omaha made no attempt to slow Emily's pace. He guided her in the direction the stranger had taken, and Emily responded instantly, enjoying her run too much to risk having it ended by disobedience. The soft muck of the riverbank had been easier on Emily's hoofs, but she did not seem to mind as they dove into the trees in hot pursuit, the aspen leaves shimmering overhead and swishing under foot.

A cry, far ahead, and quickly stifled, drifted back to Omaha and blended with the soft, rhythmic hoofbeats of a running horse. Then, abruptly, all sound stopped. Silence, except for Emily's own hoofbeats and the soft whisper of the wind through the trees, settled over him. The stranger, having seen Emily bearing down on him even before he had snatched Cinnamon from the water, and riding double now to boot, had obviously pulled up somewhere hoping to lose his pursuer.

Grimly, Omaha pressed on, his eyes scanning the fast-moving earth at Emily's feet for some sign, not knowing whether he should press for speed to run the stranger down, or slow to a walk to track him.

CHAPTER NINE

Many were the times in Omaha Jones' life when he had made mistakes, but this was one he regretted more than most. He had pressed for speed, pushing Emily, counting on eyes that he had thought as sharp as any eagle's to pick up some sign of where Cinnamon and her captor had dodged off the trail. But now he had to admit to himself that he had lost them. Riding double the way

116

they had been, Emily would have been able to run them down had he chosen the right direction. The trouble was, he had seen nothing. Nothing had seemed disturbed, nothing to indicate a trail had been covered quickly to hide it from his eyes. The facts meant he was going to have to backtrack. He was going to have to pick up the horse's tracks back near the river and unravel the trail from there. That was going to take time, and each passing minute was undoubtedly putting more distance between them. The only bright spot was the fact that Omaha was a good tracker and would find them, but he was not sure what he was going to do when he did. First, he had to let Griz and Otto know what had happened. He was not bargaining for having Griz yelling horse thief all over the countryside and pointing a finger in his direction. Besides, with the mule and Otto's colt to consider, they would not be able to move along very fast in Omaha's wake. What Omaha had to do would take time, and the short amount it would take to get back to Griz and Otto would make no marked difference.

Omaha sent Emily along at a gallop, spotting the first traces of a trail left by Cinnamon and the stranger near the river, and he sidestepped them carefully to avoid disturbing them. By the time Griz and Otto came into view, they had already covered better than half the distance between the place where they had forded the river and where Cinnamon had been snatched. Griz was riding Cinnamon's pony with the mule on lead, and Otto was astride his mare, his arms full of colt. As he galloped toward them they both stared at him with unanswered questions written across their faces. The fact that Cinnamon was not with him was self-evident and the only conclusion they would reach was that she had been drowned before he could reach her. When Cinnamon had been taken from the water by the stranger they had been well out of their vision.

'What happened?' Griz, still sodden and dripping with his every move, demanded of Omaha as Emily's excited prancing brought him back in bellowing range.

Otto's face was very sad as he awaited the news he expected to hear. 'She is lost?' Otto almost stated it instead of asking it.

Omaha shook his head. 'She didn't drown,' he told both of them. 'Last I saw of her, she wasn't happy, or comfortable, but she sure was alive and out of the river. Someone beat me to her. Rode out of the trees, pulled her out of the river, and rode off with her.'

'Was it that fella she's been runnin' from?' Griz's face was suffused with a red flush of rage.

'I think so,' Omaha admitted, 'but I wasn't close enough to be sure or Emily and I would have caught them.'

'I'll kill the varmint!' Griz proclaimed. 'If he hurts that little gal I'll do worse'n kill 'im!'

'Kill!' Otto asked blankly, unaware of the situation, or the circumstances that had thrown the odd trio together before his own unplanned addition to the group. 'Kill? Who?' Otto asked, his words thickly accented, his gaze wandering questioningly from one man to another.

'We have to catch up to them first,' Omaha threw at Griz, ignoring Otto at his elbow. 'Almost had them right at the start, but whoever it is must be about as crafty as that puma you've been tracking. He slipped off to the side and let me ride right past him.'

'You're already sittin' the fastest horse in many a territory,' Griz growled sourly. 'Get yourself moving!'

Nodding curtly, Omaha wheeled Emily to go back and pick up the trail where he had seen it branch off. 'I'll mark a trail for you to follow,' he called back over his shoulder.

'Ain't necessary,' Griz shot back. 'I can track a fly across water.'

Omaha was off at a gallop, going back over now familiar ground when Otto turned to Griz, a picture of puzzlement as if this new land completely baffled him. When those around him spoke slow, clear English he

119

could understand fairly well, but at times such as these, he felt as if he understood nothing. Track a fly across water? Otto sighed. Life would be much easier when he rejoined the wagon train he had left when he found his mare was to foal soon. Several mule skinners with the wagons spoke the language of his homeland. But, in spite of the language problem, Otto Kranz found himself feeling more as one with the broad wild country that surrounded him with each day. He had chosen to stay with his horse when he could have abandoned her and ridden on in safety with the wagons. It was a thing such a man as Griz would have done, and Otto had been thoroughly pleased with himself in spite of the risk he had taken of ending up with a dead horse and on foot in wild country, alone. In this country, Otto had come to learn, a horse meant as much to a man as life itself, mainly because without a horse he was likely to end up dead.

Otto gazed after Omaha's retreating form. He liked the girl Cinnamon very much. The whole situation puzzled Otto and he wondered what had caused it. Someone had been following her, he had understood that much from what Griz had said. And now, suddenly, she was gone. Otto, though, had come to understand some of Omaha's abilities since they had joined up together. The breed, what Griz called him, would find

Cinnamon and bring her back safely ... he hoped. At least from what Griz had told him, that was the way it seemed it should work. According to Griz, Omaha was half wild Indian and while Otto knew nothing of the individual tribes, and could recognize little of the Indian in Omaha, he had noted that the Indians he had heard about and the few he had come across, had always had an almost unnerving way of getting to the root of the matter at the outset.

The wind rippling the ill-fitting shirt Griz had given him, Omaha pressed on following the trail he had picked up near the riverbank. Whoever the man was he was following, he was cagey, and he was up on a mighty fine horse. It might not be the fastest one in a lot of territories, but it had staying power, and carrying a double load at that. For a time, while Omaha was feeling the man out, figuring the way he thought, he lost the trail time and again. Then he started to see the pattern. And with the recognition of the way the man's mind worked came the second-guessing, the anticipating of his next move. Omaha did not know the country as the man ahead of him with Cinnamon obviously did, but he did know how to track, and finally he was gaining ground on his so far elusive quarry.

There were few signs of Cinnamon along the way, except for her small bootprints where both she and the stranger had gotten off the horse to walk it for a way. Beyond that there was nearly nothing. She obviously was not trying to leave a trail for anyone to follow. She had to be *expecting* him to follow, didn't she?

That night Omaha had a cold, dry camp. Knowing he was close behind Cinnamon and her abductor, he could not risk a fire, and not being anywhere near water, both he and Emily had to make do with the contents of his canteen. Omaha leaned back against Emily's saddle where he had thrown it after removing it from her back to give her a rest, and pondered the situation. Water was not a problem in that country. They would come across some when they hit the trail again. And food could wait. Plenty of jerky was in Emily's pack, put there by Griz when they had started out from the dugout. Griz was a great believer in being ready for anything. All the animals carried a poke of jerky and hardtack and each had a spare canteen slung over the saddle horn. Griz was so canny he even managed to carry an extra stash of provisions hidden somewhere beneath the pelts that draped around his massive shoulders.

Restless as he stared up at the inky night sky, Omaha thought of Cinnamon and the man who had pulled her from the river. They could not be far ahead, but nighttime was not the time for tracking. The man with her was far from inexperienced. Even in the daylight his trail was not an easy one to follow. On a night like this, the clouds blotting the shine of the stars from the sky and the moon nowhere in evidence, it would be impossible to do anything more than get himself lost. Had he been where he had roamed the hills and canyons since he was a boy he could have probably done more. Omaha was a stranger to this land and as it was, there was nothing he could do but wait. He could not even take solace in the fact that the man with Cinnamon would have to do the same, because if he knew the land well, he would not. Emily's speed, though, was to his advantage as well as the fact that the abductor and Cinnamon had only one horse between them. Knowing Cinnamon, and having had the momentary glimpse of her determined struggle with the rider when he had gone into the river after her, Omaha did not imagine that it could be a very comfortable ride for either of them.

With a sigh, Omaha stretched out on the hard ground, his head propped against the saddle as against a pillow and let himself drift off while Emily cropped grass from the small patch where he had her picketed.

Omaha catnapped, jerking awake at every night sound through most of the night. In the past he had been on much more dangerous trails and never had reacted in such a way. Always, he had been able to drop almost instantly into a deep restful sleep, even for short periods of time. Nothing about this night, though, was the same as before, and Omaha had neither the time nor the inclination to analyze why.

With the first faint rays of the morning light, Omaha was again astride Emily, her effortless strides carrying him swiftly through a stand of pines that covered the west slope of a mountain that rose majestically from the surrounding terrain. The trail seemed to become fresher with each passing moment. For some reason Cinnamon and the man had not pressed on through the night as Omaha had feared they would. Nothing about the tracks of the horse indicated it had gone lame or that there was any reason for their lack of progress. Omaha wondered about it, but he did not have to wonder long.

As he watched the trail unfold at Emily's feet, Omaha slowed her to an uneven, hesitant walk. Suddenly, something clicked. A warning went off far in the back of Omaha's mind, but unfortunately he chose that time to ignore it.

'Your soul is already damned to perdition for what you did!' a deep resonant voice thundered behind Omaha. 'Your soul will burn throughout eternity. You just stay real still or I'll be sending your soul to hell before you'd planned on going. Raise your hands above your head,' the voice snapped.

Startled out of his concentration, Omaha obeyed, still having seen nothing of the man who held him. The double click of a shotgun being drawn back to full cock behind him had been enough to convince Omaha of the wisdom of his co-operation, at least for the moment. He could almost feel the itch along his spine where the shotgun was pointing. Omaha felt like a fool, his arms outstretched toward the heavens, Emily's reins dangling from one hand as she shifted nervously beneath her saddle, sensing the tension that shot through Omaha like lightning splitting the sky before a storm. Tossing her head repeatedly, she nervously lifted her feet and placed them back on the ground in what was almost a dance as Omaha tried to control the high-strung animal with the pressure in his legs and light tugs on the reins from his outstretched hand.

'Now turn and face me, son of Satan,' the voice demanded. 'You dare to follow us!' the voice thundered as Omaha swung Emily in a slow turn, and got his first good look at the body attached to the voice. 'You *dare* to follow us into the wilderness after what you have done!'

Omaha's eyes swept the man, tall and thin with a long horse face shadowed by several days' growth of black beard, the dark

125

brooding look heightened by thin compressed lips that were etched in a deep condemning frown. Brown hair, thick and wavy, stood out from his scalp in a snarled tangle, adding to the gleam of the fanatic that lit brooding brown eyes. He was dressed in black from head to toe including the flat-crowned hat that sat squarely on his head. The only break in the somber color that included boots and six-gun tucked in the waistband of his pants, was the dingy gray collar at his throat that must have been white at some time in the dim past. A preacher? Omaha's eyes completed their quick appraisal, then stopped and focused on the shotgun cradled carelessly in the man's arms. The stranger looked like a preacher to Omaha, and sounded like one the way he was carrying on.

While Omaha had been evaluating him, the man had been doing the same to him, and when he was finished his face was a fiery red behind the whiskers that darkened it, his eyes flashing with righteous rage. There was a moment when all Omaha could see was the slight tightening of the stranger's finger on both triggers of the cocked shotgun. Then, after a long moment of silence that seemed somehow unnatural, he appeared to regain control of himself.

'You are indeed the daughter of the devil!' he breathed vehemently. 'Your sin was bad

126

enough, but now I find you did it with a heathen.' His voice was tightly controlled, but it did not seem as if it could last long. '*This* is the father of the child you carry? This is the man you snuck away from the house to lay with like a common trollop? Oh, you are surely your mother's daughter!'

Until he had addressed her, Omaha had been unaware of Cinnamon's presence though he had assumed she would have to be somewhere nearby. There was something about a double-barreled shotgun that always had held his undivided attention. Especially when it was fully cocked and aimed at him. His gaze shifted to where she stood unfettered beside a tree with the horse tied beyond her. The words the preacher spoke jarred Omaha out of his own thoughts about what to do about the situation.

'Now, you just hold on.' Omaha started to protest his fatherhood of anyone's child, and certainly not Cinnamon's. 'I'm not...'

'Silence!' Cinnamon's rescuer-abductor roared as if addressing the heavens. 'It is *her* soul I am trying to save. Yours is already lost and beyond hope. If you were not the father of the child she carries, I would strike you down right here and now!'

Cinnamon looked a bit pale when she caught Omaha's eyes, but other than that she was the picture of innocence. Her blue eyes were wide and round, her lips slightly parted and a red blush touched her apple cheeks, making the rest of her face seem even more pale. Without success, Omaha was trying to determine whether she was acting or was indeed as frightened as she looked. With the raving maniac that confronted them both, shotgun still at full cock, if she was not frightened, she had to be every bit as crazy as he, or more to the point, know who he was and what to expect from him. He was the man who had been following her, the man she had run from with so many lies and such determination. Omaha could see her point if not condone her methods.

Shifting his weight in the saddle, Omaha prepared to take some action of his own. He glanced quickly around, uncertain as to how the crazy preacher had managed to get himself into position to ambush him without his being aware of it, but sure he was not going to make any similar mistakes now.

'I'm not...' Omaha tried to get his message across once again as he tensed, ready for what he had to do, jump a man with a loaded, fully cocked shotgun.

'Silence, Infidel!' the man exploded, waving the shotgun with far too much intensity for Omaha to try what he planned. 'I, Jethro Clayton made a vow at this girl's mother's deathbed that I would take care of her, keep her pure until she married one day far in the future. I might have taken her to wife myself, but now you, you and those greasy companions of yours have changed all that.'

Omaha shot a glance in Cinnamon's direction and thought he caught her gazing thankfully up toward the heavens.

'She has run away from me before, it's the devil's work, but never before with these results,' Jethro claimed, shaking with rage, his fanatical eyes fastened on Omaha with an accusing, damning look.

In the first place, not for one minute did Omaha believe that Cinnamon was in the family way, and in the second, all he wanted to do was fly. Why then, he could not help glancing heavenward himself, did he keep getting mixed up in these things when he had nothing to do with them, and was even less interested in their outcome? Well, that last part was not quite true. He was interested in the outcome, considering it could mean his hide added to the fact that he had come to rescue Cinnamon and could not leave her here now that he had found her.

'Her mother was a whore, did she tell you that?' Jethro raved on. 'My father married her and took her and her daughter Cinnamon away from that life. My father was a good man who forgave the past as I myself shall if Cinnamon repents for her sins.'

Cinnamon paled again, and Omaha could

almost sense rather than actually see her edging with deceptive slowness toward the tethered horse, keeping one eye on Jethro the whole time. She had a determined set to her face and did not look ready to repent for anything.

'She was always a dreamer, Cinnamon was.' Jethro weighed each word heavily as if that in itself were a mortal sin. 'I should have known it would come to this. I should have married her when she turned sixteen and taken her to me then.'

Cinnamon's face had a sour look, her full red lips turned down at the corners. She looked as if she wanted to throw up. Jethro's face, though, was a study of tightly controlled lust beneath that seething exterior of fanaticism.

'Did you think,' Jethro roared, 'that I would permit you to marry? That because of the child I would allow such a travesty? Well, you're wrong!' He answered his own question, bellowing with all the verve of a mule skinner. 'Your reward for your deed shall be a sound thrashing, and a warning. After this, if I ever see you near Cinnamon again I shall not hesitate to pull this trigger. Now, get off of that horse and take what's coming to you!'

Omaha had given up trying to protest against Jethro Clayton's tirade, but he was more than happy to oblige his demand to step down out of the saddle. Omaha Jones had never been known as a fair fighter, and now was certainly not the time to start. He had always believed it was not how you fought, but who won that counted. With a wild war whoop, Omaha launched himself from the leather like an arrow in flight, catching Jethro about his narrow shoulders in a headlong drive to the ground. The shotgun exploded with a reverberating roar that felt as if it cracked Omaha's eardrums. Then the gun went spinning off into the trees beyond Emily's feet.

Locked together like a pair of bull moose with their antlers entwined, they hit the ground, each grappling madly with the other, seeking a weak spot in the other that would allow him to be pinned. Omaha could feel the sinewy strength of his opponent beneath his black frock, see the wild light in his eyes as they twisted and turned in each other's grasp, their faces only inches apart.

To Jethro's way of thinking, he was grappling with the devil himself, fighting for a soul, and he was determined not to lose. He was not prepared to admit the devil's superiority in any form.

Jerking one hand free, Omaha landed a sharp jab to Jethro's midsection that snatched his breath away and made his red face go chalky white. For a moment he wheezed, then, fending off another blow, he clamped Omaha in a bear hug and rolled on top of him with suffocating force. His arms pinned to his sides helplessly, Omaha started butting his head against Jethro's chest with the force of a charging bull buffalo. It did not take long for the pounding to break Jethro's grip, and for the first time since Omaha had left Emily's back, they rolled apart. Just as quickly though, like a pair of fighting tomcats, they were back together again. They had not yet even managed to gain their feet before they were rolling together in a mad melee beneath the canopy the trees' branches provided overhead.

Abruptly, Jethro got the leverage and threw Omaha over his head. Omaha landed flat on his back, the breath knocked out of him for a moment, and Jethro lunged for him like a leaping cougar. At the last instant, Omaha caught sight of his blurred form out of the corner of his eye and threw himself into a sideways roll to avoid the pummeling body as it crashed down toward him. Jethro missed his jump and plowed into the ground with bone-jarring force.

Emily sidestepped swiftly, her ears flicked forward in curiosity, and Cinnamon had a sudden change in plan. She had been edging her way back toward Jethro's horse until Emily swung suddenly her way. Jethro's horse was certainly a good one, but nowhere near as swift as Emily, and Cinnamon knew that for a fact. And, at the moment, there was not much on Cinnamon's mind that had to do with right and wrong, all she was thinking about was getting away. With that one thought foremost in her dreamer's way of thinking and analyzing there seemed nothing wrong with the idea of climbing up on the back of the fastest horse, and clearing out while she had the chance. She did not particularly want to risk the possibility of Jethro winning while she just stood there with her mouth hanging open. Cinnamon Clayton had many other things she wanted to do besides end up hopelessly tied to a self-ordained fanatic who liked to think of himself as a preacher, which he was not. He had merely donned the frock one day and picked up the fight against sin, which he associated in most cases with women in some way or another. The gospel, according to Jethro Clayton, could be summed up in his one basic belief that all the troubles in the world somehow either directly or indirectly were caused by and put forth by women exclusively. Women did the corrupting, men were merely the victims. That of course excluded heathen non-believers, who were all rotten to the very core of their beings, and Omaha, by virtue of his half-Indian blood would be considered even more of a lowlife than herself. She, at least, had a few redeeming qualities in Jethro's opinion.

Omaha had none. Cinnamon did not think she had the time to see whether good would triumph over evil or the other way around, in spite of the fact that she was rooting for evil.

The fight continued without letup, the two men grappling with each other, neither giving an inch, while Cinnamon edged her way to where Emily stood patiently waiting and stepped lightly into the saddle. With a gentle hand, she turned her and started her at a walk away from the brawling pair, hoping not to draw their attention as she left. What she had been hoping for, though, was too much. Cinnamon was barely mounted and moving when Omaha, sprawled amongst the leaves, with Jethro astride him pounding away with both bony hard fists, caught the movement out of the corner of his eye. Since he had met Griz, Emily was never very far from his thoughts, and now was not an exception.

'Cinnamon!' Omaha yelled through rapidly swelling lips. With a heave he rolled from beneath Jethro and made a lunge to gain his feet, the fight suddenly seeming less important than losing the horse.

Jethro was not of the same opinion and he moved like a cat. With one swift movement from the ground, he rolled over and his hand shot out like a cat's paw, snagging Omaha about the ankle, again jerking his feet out from under him, and throwing him to the earth as Cinnamon, in a panic, touched her heels to Emily and raced out of there like she had to make Wyoming by morning.

'Cinnamon!' Omaha tried again, but it was plain nothing was going to stop her.

Catching a quick glimpse of a shapely leg and flying skirts as Emily hit her full stride, Omaha was once again entangled with Jethro Clayton, battling now just to be free of him so he could go after Cinnamon. Staggering to their feet, braced in combat like a pair of enraged bears, neither one could free himself enough to take a swing at the other.

Locked together, they staggered back and forth across the small clearing, Omaha pulling toward Jethro's horse, and Jethro pulling away. Both faces were red as a cloudy sunset with teeth clenched tightly as they exchanged close-up snarls and matching epithets. As they were staggering together again across the clearing, Omaha's eye caught sight of where the bluff dissolved in a sharp drop of several feet, ending in a scattering of rocks that had made up the lip of the bluff before some act of nature had collapsed it. As they neared it, one grudging step at a time, Omaha got an idea. It was certainly not a very good one, but it was the only one he could come up with right then. He had to break Jethro's grip before he could go after Cinnamon, who, by virtue of her custody of Emily, was much more important than anything Jethro might have on his mind.

Still pressed together like a pair of canned sardines as they neared the cutaway bluff, Omaha let Jethro turn him as they struggled together, relinquishing his stand only an inch or two at a time until they were standing, without Jethro's knowing it, at the precipice.

Omaha feinted a backwards slip. Jethro pressed him. Omaha went rigid, his muscles locked as if they were steel bands as Jethro threw himself against Omaha again, Jethro's own weight working against him. The jarring force of his lunge broke loose their footing on the rocky bluff and without even an instant to reconsider, they were both plummeting into empty space, Omaha's face touched by a grim little smile of satisfaction.

For an instant it seemed as if time froze and there ensued an even more frantic, but barely discernible battle between the two combatants. In midair they fought and struggled, in a bizarre, silent test of strength. Muscle against muscle, faces set in tight pinched masks of flesh as each fought his battle to end up on top when they crashed into the earth that rushed up to meet them.

Seconds passed like hours as, each locked in the other's grip, they fell, and at the last possible instant, Omaha felt Jethro roll beneath him as the ground came up to slam into them like a gigantic fist. Jethro groaned,

136

his grip on Omaha relaxed.

Omaha disengaged himself from his breathless sprawl on top of Jethro Clayton and rolled to his feet, gazing down at the supine form. He was out cold, and Omaha hoped he would stay that way for a time. Then, with a determined set to his jaw, Omaha scrambled back up the loose slope they had bypassed on their way down and directed his feet toward where Jethro's horse still waited patiently where it was tethered among the trees.

Horse thievery seemed to be contagious when someone was around Cinnamon very long. Jethro's was the only horse around, and Omaha knew he had to get Emily back. That left him with no other choice, and he could not even say he regretted the situation. A nice long walk might do something to cool Jethro off, but, Omaha mused as he climbed into the saddle, he doubted it.

CHAPTER TEN

'Kingman's camp ain't hardly a half a day's ride from here,' Griz flung over his shoulder at Otto as he continued to examine the place where Omaha and Jethro had had their disagreement earlier that day.

In the fading light of day, Griz was able to

read in the fresh tracks almost everything that had happened between Omaha, Cinnamon, and the stranger Omaha had set out after. Otto stayed mounted and watched with keen interest as Griz prowled the area, muttering to himself most of the time as he did. Ezra had come up to join them, panting from a run he had taken in pursuit of a rabbit, and immediately turned his attention to what Griz was investigating, sniffing and snuffling in short little arcs, crisscrossing the clearing and bluff area. Pretty soon the coyote, his curiosity satisfied, sat down at the edge of the trees, threw his head back, and cut loose with an unearthly howl as the sun set and the moon rose with a glimmering light above the treetops.

It was about then that Griz discovered the tracks he disapproved of heartily. He stared at them more closely. He had followed the heavier burdened horse's tracks, and Emily's. He bad seen the signs of a fight, and seen where Cinnamon had stationed herself a safe distance away to watch. What Griz found now were Cinnamon's small bootprints leading up to Emily's hoofprints and the disappearance of Cinnamon's tracks where Emily's sank a bit deeper into the soft earth. Cinnamon was riding Emily, alone. There were signs to show that the other horse had been mounted by Omaha and sent off at a gallop in the same direction

Cinnamon had taken. And also tracks of a lone man who had followed, on foot, some time later, originating from the base of the bluff, where he had apparently fallen with Omaha, Omaha being the only one to emerge unscathed.

The fact that Omaha was following Cinnamon meant that he did not know where she was and that brought to Griz's mind only one foremost question. Where was Emily?

As the sunset faded from its blazing oranges and yellows into the dim gray-black of night, Griz swore with great gusto. He swore at the mule that had continually slowed them, and he swore at Ezra, who kept up his howling at the rising moon.

By now, accustomed to Griz's querulous nature, Otto climbed down from his mare and started to set up camp as they did each night with the setting of the sun. Making progress after dark was almost impossible, and unless one knew where he was going, there was the double risk of getting lost as well. That was Griz Tanner's own wise philosophy, but this night he was not in the mood for wisdom or philosophy. Emily was missing. The horse was no longer in Omaha's care, where he had placed her. He could hardly believe that Cinnamon had stolen her, and if he had not seen the tracks with his own eyes he would not have believed it, but the proof lay right at his feet, and there was no denying it.

Then, suddenly, a small smile crept across Griz's grim countenance. He had said it himself to Otto only minutes before. Kingman's camp was only a few hours away. The tracks were heading in that direction, all of them. Including the ones on foot. Kingman's camp was the mining camp where Griz had planned on having Emily's first race. It was one of the biggest mining camps Griz had ever been in, and barring the end of the strike it would still be there, probably bigger and better than ever. That's where they would all be, and that was where they had to be.

'Pack up,' Griz growled, 'we're pulling out.'

In the midst of gathering firewood Otto stared hard at Griz for a moment, but Ezra, used to the ring of the familiar words, broke his stance with muzzle pointed toward the sky and lit out, ranging far ahead of where Griz and Otto would follow. Certain that life would be much easier when he again located the pack train he had quit for his horse, Otto began to repack the mule without a word of protest. Griz was a man experienced in this country. He was not. Otto Kranz was a patient man, willing to put up with another's peculiarities for the knowledge he would gain along the way. The mule skinners he had been traveling with had had a lot in common with Griz. They had been loud, coarse, and often ill tempered, but their advice had been sound, their knowledge seemingly endless. A stranger to this land could learn a lot from that breed of man if he was patient and listened. In spite of that, Otto had to admit to himself that there were times when he would much rather learn his lessons about the new country he had come to from Omaha Jones, the young man Griz referred to often as the breed. Instinctively, Otto knew there was something less than complimentary in the address that Griz used, though coming from Griz it did not seem so. And Omaha had never given anything more than a grumbled objection. It was, Otto deduced, an insult when used at large, but an accepted address between the two men. It was plain to Otto that he was going to have to have a far greater mastery of this strange new language before he understood all that passed between the men, or the women, for that matter. Cinnamon had been a complete mystery to him the short time he had had to get to know her. And, now, they were all determined to rescue her from whatever fate had befallen her after her dunking in the river. The men in this land were a stalwart lot, Otto decided, much like himself. He would have no trouble growing with the vast land that rolled to great distances far beyond

141

where the eye could see.

Like a man possessed, Griz set out on the trail he had discovered. Where Otto could not even see the suggestion of a trail, Griz picked out a stray hoof or bootprint in the faint moonlight and they plodded on. The pace was not fast in deference to the mule as well as Otto's mare and new foal. The weight of Griz Tanner perched on Cinnamon's tough little pony was also a consideration. Still they moved on, the miles grinding out from beneath dragging hoofs and tired feet. What Otto did not realize about Griz's great tracking ability was the fact that he had already known where they were heading before they had taken out after the others though the sun had set, leaving them in darkness. The stray hoof or bootprint he managed to discern along the way only confirmed what he had already accepted as fact. Those they were following were all heading as the crow flies straight for Kingman's camp. Cinnamon was plainly in the lead. All that puzzled Griz was the question about whether she had known of the camp's existence or if dumb luck had been the driving force that had sent her alone in that direction. And why, Griz pondered, had she taken Emily? Kingman's camp was no Sunday social. It was as raw and wild an encampment, or town, or whatever anyone wanted to call it, as the West ever bred. A

142

girl with Cinnamon's looks and a horse like Emily would not last ten minutes on the street before someone made a grab for one or the other or both. In his care, Griz had never had to worry about Emily, but in the hands of such a frail flower as Cinnamon there would very quickly be an ownership dispute that the law, such as it was, would have no part in.

Chewing thoughtfully on some jerky, Griz gazed pensively down on the lights of Kingman's camp where they glowed far below. Before pressing on they had paused on the crest of the green hill, giving the animals a breather. Through most of the night they had traveled and into the wee hours of the morning. In a very short time dawn would be streaking the eastern sky with shafts of light that seemed to be reaching for the heavens. The faint trail that Griz had been catching glimpses of all along his trek had disappeared completely now into the heavy spring grasses of the meadow bordering Kingman's camp in a vast sweeping arc that rolled away from the pine-forested heart of the encampment. Lights flickered between the trees with an almost welcoming pulse.

Ezra's ears flicked forward and his nose twitched as he caught sight, sound, and smell of man. Suddenly he appeared none too eager to range ahead of his companions

143

and press on. The sights and sounds of men other than Griz seemed always to signal trouble. Ezra reverted to the coyote slink and sat down quietly to one side, his tail curled beneath him, his head drooping.

With a sudden grunt that apparently did not mean much of anything, Griz climbed up on the back of Cinnamon's pony and led the way down the easy slope toward the camp. Without a word Otto followed, the foal on lead for a change, the mule keeping pace ahead, Omaha's wings making it appear as a bizarre four-legged buzzard that could not get off the ground. As they approached the outskirts of the camp Ezra stayed close by Griz's side.

It had been hours before, barely dusk, when Omaha Jones had passed the way Griz and Otto passed near sunrise. In his haste to be after Cinnamon astride Emily, he had not bothered to cover his trail, knowing it would take some time for Jethro Clayton to follow them on foot. He was just as sure, though, that Jethro would follow. And Cinnamon had come into Kingman's camp in a beeline, just like a homing pigeon coming home. Had she known of the tent town's presence? Her actions seemed to indicate that she had. It had to be the only settlement of any kind for miles.

When Omaha had crested the hill overlooking Kingman's camp from the east, he had noticed something familiar about the place. He knew he had seen it before, but had been unable to place it until he remembered the details of his first eventful flight. He had flown over it. Omaha was dead sure there could be no other such as Kingman's camp anywhere near where his flight path had taken him. There was a uniqueness about the gash in the thick forest crowded by tents and wood-framed tents as well as the gaping openings where the miners plunged into the earth in the surrounding hills that could hardly be matched elsewhere. There was an atmosphere, a feeling for rough work, and even rougher play peppered with an almost childlike curiosity. Kingman's camp provided a brutal head-on meeting of life on something more than its own terms that would be difficult to duplicate. This was the camp where men had abandoned their interest in a fight to follow him over the far hills as if he had been an airborne pied piper.

Almost from the moment he hit the main street of Kingman's camp, Omaha was sure he was not very far behind Cinnamon. There was a stirring in the street, an electricity in the air. A girl such as Cinnamon, handling a horse such as Emily, would have caused quite a stir in passing. And, to Omaha's experience, Kingman's camp was showing all the signs of beginning a wild night. He wondered as he walked Jethro's horse down the middle of the main street, if it was Saturday.

Drawing his own share of stares, Omaha let the reins dangle loosely, having identified the horse he rode as one with plenty of staying power and certainly his share of speed, but little spirit. Lights were going on all up and down the street and well into the distance as lanterns and lamps were lit to keep the darkness at bay while the miners' spirits warmed and began taking on new dimensions as the night settled in.

Omaha was wary. He was only too well aware of his own strange appearance in his ceremonial beaded leggings, moccasins, and oversized plaid shirt Griz had given him. And he was aware of the six-gun, feeling the weight where it rode at his hip, knowing in a town of this sort a man who wore one had better be able to use it.

Kingman's camp consisted of one saloon, gambling house, or red light establishment after another. The men who walked its infrequent boardwalks and muddy streets were split almost fifty-fifty between ebullient miners with arms the size of melons and hands with the gripping force of a vise, and trim, nattily dressed dandies who ran the sporting houses. The vast majority of the ladies were dressed in spangles, beads, and short skirts revealing much more than a demure ankle. The few that were not, were

146

dressed in plain cottons and gazed fixedly ahead with studied coolness as they had gone about their business of getting home before the sun set. After dark proper ladies were not to be seen anywhere. For the most part, Omaha could feel feminine eyes on him as he passed. When he met the gazes with his own eyes, he found them to be bold and inviting.

Lights burned bright on the streets, leaving the only dark corners in alleyways between the tents and behind them. Piano music poured out of one establishment along with its flood of bright light that lit the street outside in a huge pool of yellow light in which miners and befeathered ladies danced. Further down the street fiddle music drifted out on the night air accompanied by a harmonica, and from somewhere the soft chords of a guitar competed with it.

Water trickled through the middle of the muddy street in a thin stream, water that heralded the coming of spring with the melting of the snow on the surrounding mountain peaks. Omaha's horse passed down the length of the street, its hoofs making soft, barely audible sucking sounds in the mud as the camp's enthusiasm built around him. As Omaha made his way down the street a fistfight broke out on the far end of the camp and was quickly surrounded by spectators. He was keeping a weather eye out for some sign of Emily's whereabouts, and

Cinnamon too, for that matter. There was no doubt in his mind that they were in the camp somewhere. Cinnamon was not too taken with the wild country surrounding them, and there was nowhere else she could have gone. Besides, the tracks had led right up to the edge of Kingman's camp before disappearing in the muck pounded down beneath the heavy traffic of horses, mules, people, and stray dogs that populated the camp.

About to give up his horseback survey and start a one-man, tent-to-tent search for Cinnamon, Omaha climbed down, his moccasins sinking deeply into the mire. The horse kept lifting his feet in an almost delicate dance as if it were afraid that if it did not keep moving, it would sink forever in the thick mud that made up the surface of the street.

A stray dog, mottled yellow and white in color, slunk by as Omaha turned and started walking, the horse on lead. He knew there would not be much time to locate Cinnamon before Jethro Clayton was sure to show up. And Omaha had no doubt that he would be no further behind than the difference in time that it took a man to follow a horse on foot. And Kingman's camp had not been a long ride. Jethro would show up well before sunrise if Omaha's brief experience with the man was anything to go by. Omaha's only fear was that Cinnamon could be much easier to locate than Emily. Still, where would a young woman hide in a raw settlement like Kingman's camp? Omaha had not yet caught sight of a reputable boarding house or a hotel that looked anything less than sleazy with a cockeyed sign dangling from the front of a wooden-framed tent structure and amply decorated inside and out with the spangled ladies. The few wooden buildings that bordered the street on either end did not look much better, and as far as Omaha had seen, housed only the general store, one saloon, a flophouse where a man could buy a bed for the night, and one home a determined miner had built for his wife, a woman who looked thoroughly capable of defending her ownership should the fact ever be disputed. Omaha had seen her twice. Once as he had crossed the street and gone up the street and then again when he came down it, and each time she had glowered at him from the porch, a rifle cozily resting across her knees.

Preparing to head up the street again, Omaha heard a soft whinny from somewhere nearby, and it had a familiar ring to it. He paused in his tracks, peering into the gloom that hovered between the tents where the light was blocked and wondered if it was his imagination. A moment later he heard another sound.

'Pssst!' a softly feminine voice drifted his way with an anxious ring. 'Over here, Omaha,' Cinnamon's voice, now recognizable, persisted.

Omaha peered down the alley uncertainly, not knowing what she had on her mind and knowing at the same time that she was certainly not among the most trustworthy people he had known. He would have to approach her carefully, but as yet he had not even seen her. Then, abruptly, a slender white hand appeared from between the tent flaps at the side of one of the more gaudy establishments that lined the muddy street. It gestured wildly for him to come closer, and he could see a tiny split in the flaps higher up where an eye was pressed against the opening, staring in his direction.

With a quick glance around to see if anyone might be paying any attention to him, Omaha stepped forward to where the hand stuck out of the tent. The instant he was within range the hand reached out and snatched his wrist, jerking him forward and into the tent. Loud music from the street continued to blare forth as Omaha stared questioningly down into Cinnamon's face while he hung onto the reins of the horse that stood just outside.

CHAPTER ELEVEN

Omaha found himself standing uncomfortably tight against Cinnamon in the close confines of the canvased-off area that apparently served as a more discreet entrance to the bawdy establishment. Leaning cozily against him, she gazed up at him out of wide innocent blue eyes and spoke in a breathless whisper.

'I told you I couldn't swim.' As if they had been parted by the chilled waters of the river and her peculiar stepbrother only minutes before, Cinnamon said the words almost accusingly.

Without uttering a sound, Omaha just looked at her, and that in itself was not easy the way her slight form was pressed so tightly against him. All too aware of the exceedingly close contact, he had to crane his neck in a tight arc to look down into her round face. Although not exactly enjoying the situation, he found it did have its pleasant aspects.

'I ... I knew you would come,' Cinnamon rushed on. 'I took Emily because I knew you would come.'

Gazing down into her face, Omaha was aware of the soft rustling of silks and satins in the background as he tried to believe her. He wanted to believe her, but somehow he just could not do it. For the moment he would settle for believing that she had hoped he would turn up instead of the fanatic who had plucked her from the river, Jethro Clayton. The man who made claim to being her stepbrother, but who had anything but brotherly intent where Cinnamon was concerned.

'What about Jethro?' Cinnamon asked to Omaha's continued silence. Her eyes grew even rounder. 'You didn't...?' She left the rest of the obvious question unasked.

'I didn't kill him,' Omaha said quickly, pushing Cinnamon back a step from him so he could get a better look at her, and almost blushing, in spite of his own past plentiful experience, when he did.

Cinnamon looked from Omaha's startled face, down along the clothes she wore, and laughed softly at his expression. 'Don't you worry about these,' she assured him. 'They're my disguise. Belle and Ginny thought it would be better if I sort of blended in around here.'

'Well, it's sure working,' Omaha said, his eyes glued on her bare shoulders, following the glow of her creamy skin to where the red satin, spangled gown barely covered her breasts. 'I certainly wouldn't mistake you for anything other than what you appear to be.' A bit edgy, his eyes continued their inspection of her almost of their own will,

152

sliding down the length of the full satin skirts to where they ended just below her knees, her legs encased in black net stockings below that. 'And who are Belle and Ginny?'

'Some old friends of my mother's.' Cinnamon tossed off the comment lightly.

Omaha sighed. What Jethro Clayton had said, then, was about as much truth as he was likely to get out of either of them. Cinnamon appeared to be more than able to fend for herself. That left Omaha with his major problem. Where was Emily?

'Where's Emily?' He put the question to Cinnamon point-blank.

'She's all right,' Cinnamon hastened to assure him. 'The man who runs this place is keeping her with his horses out back. I told him she belonged to Griz Tanner and that he would be along in a day or so.' She smiled confidentially. 'He knows Griz, and I don't think he would let anything happen to his horse. But I don't think you better try to get her though. The fella who runs this place takes his responsibilities real serious. He just might take you for a horse thief. I hear there are plenty of them around here. And besides, he keeps a guard posted on his own stock.'

'Hey, kid, Cinnamon, where are you?' a feminine voice called softly from the other side of the canvas wall.

'In here,' Cinnamon replied in a matched low tone.

A moment later a head, piled high with soft glistening brown curls, poked through the flap and glanced uncertainly in Cinnamon's direction, ignoring Omaha as if he were a fence post. 'You all right, honey?'

Omaha took more notice of her, seeing a face, no longer young, but still attractive, and not nearly so heavily caked with powder and lip rouge as many others of her profession. While there was a hard look about the hazel eyes when they turned on Omaha, there was a different attitude altogether when they were turned on Cinnamon.

'I'm fine, Belle,' Cinnamon said roguishly. 'He's a friend.'

'I wouldn't bet on that if I were you,' Belle said with wry humor. 'I haven't met one yet who was.' She smiled sweetly in Omaha's direction as she cast a slur on the entire male sex.

'You lay a finger on that girl,' Belle addressed Omaha, 'without her wanting you to,' she quickly qualified her statement, 'and I'll have Hugo break your head,' she promised before she disappeared back the way she had come.

'Hugo is Mr Sloane's bouncer,' Cinnamon told Omaha with a nervous little laugh. 'And Belle is an old friend of my mother's.'

'Well, you better keep the bouncer close. Jethro should be showing up sometime tomorrow.'

Cinnamon gave a small gasp and sprang into Omaha's arms as if she had been launched. 'Didn't you even tie him up or something?' she asked, clinging to him. Then she buried her face in Omaha's chest, feeling the soft grittiness of flannel against her skin. 'You're not going to let him find me again!?' she cried into the shirt, her voice muffled against the cloth.

Omaha found himself suddenly holding her, and stroking her hair with a comforting hand, at the same time discovering that it was not such an unpleasant chore. And when she turned her face up to him, eyes closed, lashes wet with teardrops, he kissed her. A long kiss that set his body to tingling.

When they parted, Cinnamon gazed up at him with a vixenish gleam in her eyes. 'You look tired,' she said lightly. 'Tie your horse out back and you can use my cot,' she said, her voice husky. Her eyes sparkled and the tears were gone as she smiled teasingly at him. A moment later she was gone, slipping almost soundlessly through the flap, headed for the rear of the wood and canvas structure where she expected to meet Omaha.

Watching her slip away, Omaha wondered at himself. When would he ever be able to read Cinnamon? Her message this time had been loud and clear, the feel of her kiss was still upon his lips, but he knew too that he was continually getting himself in deeper. Ducking through the flap where he had entered, Omaha led the horse he still held to the back of the establishment, the raucous sound of drunken laughter blending with a distant banging of a piano and the closer strains of someone singing along with the discordant strains of a guitar. He knew what he should do after going without sleep for going on two nights, but he knew even better what he wanted.

With a nod in the direction of the dark silhouette that could only have been the guard tending the livestock, Omaha tied the horse he had borrowed from Jethro Clayton to the rail of the corral and turned his attention to the rear entrance of the brightly lit sporting house. The back flap rippled where there was no air to stir it, and Omaha stepped quickly forward to join Cinnamon where she held the flap open for him to pass inside. Silently she led the way down a long hall between canvas rooms, finally slipping into one that was only a few up from the back of the building. Omaha gave a what-the-hell shrug and followed her.

Inside, it was much more than Omaha had expected in consideration of Cinnamon's offhanded remark about her cot. An oil lamp burned softly in the corner of the cubicle, casting flickering shadows along the canvas walls. What Cinnamon had referred to as her cot was actually a bed made from fat timbers lashed together to four legs that looked like small stumps. A fat straw mattress lay atop a tightly woven set of rope springs. In a mining camp such as he had observed Kingman's camp to be, it was pure luxury.

'Well, here we are,' Cinnamon said lightly, smiled sweetly, and disappeared back through the room's tent-flap doorway.

Stunned, Omaha stared after her a moment. He could not have been that wrong about what he had read in her eyes and the way she had looked. Had she suddenly changed her mind? Or had she been lying again, but in a much more subtle way? Puzzled, Omaha shook his head and started to undress. He might as well get some rest while he was there. There would be plenty for him to worry about within the next few hours. Griz, he felt sure, would not be far behind Jethro Clayton, if he did not in fact catch up with him before they reached the camp.

Stripping off the ceremonial leggings he had not shed since his momentous launch from El Capitan, as well as the voluminous shirt Griz had given him, Omaha slid down between what passed for a sheet, and the heavy quilt. He had not lain on a soft bed since he had been in school back East so long ago. Omaha was aware, as he settled down and felt the heaviness in his eyelids, of the sounds of footsteps in the hall between the cubicles, and voices, full of whiskey and good humor. His head cradled in his hands, Omaha watched the canvas roof far above waffle and bubble as the soft mountain breezes blew continually against it.

He was about to drift off into velvet black oblivion when Cinnamon appeared as she had disappeared, like a mist on the wind. But now she was a different Cinnamon than when she had left. Her hair was loose, hanging softly about her face, its limp mousiness making her blue eyes seem even larger and giving her a waiflike appearance. The way the dressing gown she now wore clung to the curves of her body did much, though, to dispel that illusion.

Not expecting her back, Omaha peered at her a moment through sleep-fogged eyes before the new situation registered on his brain.

'Oh,' Cinnamon teased softly, her lips brushing his ear as she bent over him, 'if you're that tired maybe I'd better go.'

Almost by reflex, Omaha's hand shot out from under the quilt, catching her firmly by the wrist, and showed no inclination to let go. Piercing gray eyes burned up into hers from beneath hooded lids and a smile quirked the corners of his lips.

'I've never been that tired,' Omaha returned, pulling her down to him.

CHAPTER TWELVE

A long, mournful howl seeming to come from not further than arm's length away shattered the stillness of the early morning and Omaha's sleep. With a start he sat bolt upright, for an instant forgetting Cinnamon still lay by his side. The howl again assailed his ears, and Omaha knew there was no mistaking its origin. Ezra.

Cinnamon, jerked awake by Omaha's sudden movement and the blast of cold air that washed over her when he sat up pulling the quilt with him destroying their cocoon of warmth, sleepily tried to follow the quilt's promise of renewed comfort. But it was already too late. The serenity was broken, and Omaha, his eyes bloodshot from lack of sleep, was already swinging his legs over Cinnamon, piling out of bed in answer to the wailing cry of the wild. If Ezra was nearby, then so was Griz. Snatching up his clothes from the floor where he had dropped them the night before, Omaha dressed with amazing speed for a man who had gotten no more than a couple of hours' sleep, and the night before that had not slept at all. If he were to admit it, Omaha was exhausted.

'What're you doing?' Cinnamon murmured sleepily as she rolled to the edge of the bed, reaching out for Omaha, wanting to pull him back to her.

'I heard Ezra howl,' Omaha told her quickly as he strapped his borrowed six-gun in place. 'Griz has to be around the camp somewhere.'

Cinnamon frowned. 'Coyotes howl around here all the time,' she said, her voice losing some of its sleepy thickness. 'How can you tell it's Ezra? We are in the wilderness, you know.' Cinnamon made a wide gesture that tumbled her off the bed in a tangle of quilt, landing with a solid thump. She let loose with a swearword Omaha would never have imagined she knew as she flailed wildly at the twist of cloth that imprisoned her.

'I know Ezra's howl,' Omaha insisted reasonably as he scooped up Cinnamon, still wrapped tightly in the quilt, and deposited her back in bed. 'You stay here and keep out of sight like Belle told you. I'll go see what I can find out. If you'll remember back you'll recall we're both horse thieves as far as Jethro and Griz can tell.' He paused at the flap leading out of the canvas cubicle, glancing back at Cinnamon with a serious look on his face. '*Are* you in the family way?' He asked the question slowly, hesitantly, as if it might be an insult.

With a shrug Cinnamon shook her head negatively. 'No, but I just had to tell Jethro *something*, and that was all I could come up

160

with quick.'

Omaha heaved a sigh of relief, though not sure why, and left. For a moment Cinnamon stared after his exit, then she snatched up her clothes and started to dress. Omaha had told her earlier that Griz and Otto had been behind Jethro. Therefore, she reasoned, if Griz was indeed in Kingman's camp already, then she had to assume that Jethro was as well. The thought did not sit well with her, but for the moment she knew it would be wiser on her part to keep somewhere close to Omaha rather than running again so soon. Still she was a bit nervous about it, and her feet had a decided itch to be moving in an opposite direction from where she knew Jethro to be.

With long purposeful strides Omaha traversed the long narrow hall to the back of the building, where he paused just inside the back flap, lifting one edge of it to get himself a good look outside before stepping through it. What he saw there made him freeze where he was, staring anxiously out at the peculiar scene before him.

There, behind one of the fanciest sporting houses in Kingman's camp stood a white-haired Indian chief, Sioux by his dress and speech, and a stranger dressed all in black save for the buckskin vest he wore and a hatband that looked like horsehair and braided silver. Omaha saw him mostly from

161

the back and caught only an occasional glimpse of the side of his face, but the way he held himself gave Omaha cause to recognize him as the back silhouette of the night before standing guard over the animals in the corral. And, from overhearing what they were saying, Omaha felt an instant dislike and mistrust of the man. They were speaking rapidly in Sioux, broken by occasional English and emphasized by sign language. What they were planning Omaha wished he had not heard. His own heritage was half Sioux though not of the same tribe as the old chief who stood there talking rationally with the hard-eyed stranger. Omaha knew only too well the continuing trouble between the white man and the red.

Shifting his position a bit, Omaha felt his elbow bump into something soft close beside him.

'What...?' Cinnamon began, but was cut off by Omaha's hand as it darted out to cover her mouth, stifling her words.

'Shhhhh,' he hissed, his gray eyes again fixed on the scene near the corral.

Cinnamon obeyed, stooping slightly to peer out the flap beneath Omaha's arm.

The two men were planning on robbing a supply train that was due to show up any time now. Evidently the dark stranger was doing all the planning and the chief was to provide the men. Even as they spoke, several scouts were out combing the surrounding countryside for some sign of the approaching supply train. The Indians, Omaha knew, would be after the whiskey the man in black continually brought up as well as whatever else they could haul off in the way of food and clothing. The man in black, though, was a different matter. What, Omaha wondered, was he after? It had to be more than whiskey and food. There was something more here than what showed on the surface. Omaha had an almost irrepressible urge to run out to the old chief and yell for him to give up this wild idea. He and his braves would take the brunt of the raid they were planning and the man in black would ride off calmly, leaving them to their fate. The cavalry would come to hunt down the Indians responsible; Omaha had seen the white man in action before. No thought would be given to the man in black. Only the old chief and his braves would be hunted down for the crime. Any peace between white man and red, when it existed at all, was tenuous at best.

Because of that conflict, it was hard for Omaha to reconcile what he knew to be fact and what he saw before his eyes. Why was this obviously distinguished chief going along with a slimy white man's plan to raid a supply train? Much of an Indian's life, especially a chief's, centered around honor, pride, and bravery. The Sioux chief standing by the corral knew as well as Omaha the possible consequences of his act, and yet he was obviously prepared to go along with it, to take the risk. Unless, as Omaha had witnessed before, the chief and his band, with the innocent ignorance of children, believed either that the cavalry would not come, or if it did, they would emerge victorious. The promise of plentiful whiskey could do much at times to make caution fly.

As the pair finished their broken discussion and the chief left, fading into the early morning shadows behind the corral, the thin dark man who guarded the corral turned full around and Omaha got his first clear look at his face. His eyes were hooded, and black as hard coal. His hair was straight, black, and hung well over his shirt collar. And his face was angular and deeply tanned with high, prominent cheekbones. Suddenly a chill ran up Omaha's spine. There was something about him. Omaha found himself staring at a face of he did not know what. Then, as he stared, Omaha saw it. The man outside was not just a black-clothed gunslick, he was Indian, or at least part Indian. The irony of it. He was, to use Griz's favorite expression, a half-breed.

Glancing around, Omaha swore softly under his breath. There was no sign of Griz or Ezra anywhere in sight. Omaha knew he had heard Ezra when he had piled out of bed. They could not be far. First, he had to locate them, then he had to do something about what the old chief had planned with the gunslick by the corral. Omaha muttered to himself about always getting himself tied in with these things when he had a quest of his own, to fly. But, for what seemed like an interminable time since he had stepped off the edge of El Capitan, it could not be helped. He had to do something. At least from what the chief had said, none of the scouts had as yet spotted the supply train's approach. That gave him some time. Time which he knew he needed to locate Griz, who, after all, still had his wings. Omaha turned to find another way out of the canvas tent when something about the corral snatched his attention back. Something was missing. He jerked back to his post as if he had been attached to a rubber band.

'What is it?' Cinnamon whispered urgently at his elbow. 'What were they saying?' she asked, having understood little of what had passed between the pair except an occasional word in English.

But Omaha was not listening to Cinnamon's question. His eyes were fastened on the spot where he had tied Jethro's horse the night before. Nothing was there now except an empty spot. Emily was, thankfully, still in the corral with the other horses, apparently gorging herself on good hay and grain. That meant Jethro had to be in camp. Evidently he had located his horse and walked off with him. Why had he not gone further and tried to locate Cinnamon and himself? When he thought of how Jethro would have found them the night before, Omaha winced. And his gun had been on the far side of the room where he had left it with his clothes.

Omaha turned again to leave, almost falling over Cinnamon. Before he did anything else he knew he had to locate Griz. Quickly he stepped around her with hardly a glance at her, and hurried on. Almost immediately he felt a sharp tugging at his sleeve as Cinnamon swung around to face him.

'Where're you going?' Cinnamon demanded. 'Never mind, I'm going with you.' Cinnamon did not miss much, and she certainly had not missed observing the absence of Jethro's horse. She knew Jethro too well to think even for an instant that he might have given up and left as soon as he had retrieved it.

'No,' Omaha said firmly, pulling her up short. 'You stay here. I'm going to find Griz, then I'll be back. I can't let you go waltzing through every sporting house and saloon in this camp looking like that.' He nodded toward the red spangled dress she had again donned.

'Oh, all right!' Cinnamon pouted. 'But you hurry back here.'

Belle suddenly appeared in the hallway, this time with an escort, giving Omaha a dark frown as he passed by her with a hurried 'Mornin', ma'am' on his lips.

Omaha began his search for Griz with no set pattern except to eliminate the boarding houses from his list. Griz could easily be in a saloon or one of the red light houses, but Omaha was sure that he would not have bothered putting up at any rooming house. Compared to the night before the streets were quiet, but business was still booming, catering to the miners who had made a good stake and were whooping it up in camp for a few days before returning to the mines in the hills for a fresh stake. Omaha pushed and elbowed his way among them, catching an occasional puzzled look for his strange attire, but gathering none of the insults concerning his birth that he had received in many towns he had spent time in as he had crossed the continent.

Fortunately Omaha did not have to go far before his search was ended. Moving up the crowded street he caught sight of Griz's mule, the wings still loaded on her back, gathering quite a crowd in front of one of the louder, gaudier saloons. And beside her was Otto's mare and her foal, growing bigger every day, standing quietly close beside her

167

in the midst of all the confusion. The one thing Omaha did not take note of as he entered the saloon was Jethro Clayton's horse standing at the hitching rail just beyond Griz's mule, mostly concealed by the crowd that had gathered to stare inquisitively at his wings.

When Omaha paused just within the swinging doors, letting his gaze sweep over the sea of faces that filled the room, he froze, then fell into a slouch, pulling his collar up high around his neck. Almost immediately he had spotted Griz, and there with him had been, by some crazy tumble of fate, Jethro Clayton. It was obvious by Griz's sociable manner and boisterous laugh that he had no idea of who the man he was talking to was. As yet Omaha had not spotted Otto, but knew he could not be far. Uneasily, he slid into a vacant chair, losing himself in the loud, ever shifting mass of humanity around him.

Equally obvious to Omaha when he stole another glance in Griz's direction was the fact that he and Jethro were nowhere near sharing the same thoughts. A grim set look froze Jethro's face, his thin compressed lips curled down at the corners to crease into a disapproving frown. As usual, his eyebrows were arched in the fanatic's curl that Omaha had come to recognize and his thin frame was animated with agitation as his arms jerked and his finger pointed heavenward, apparently invoking the Lord's wrath. He and Griz had managed to draw quite a crowd around them. Griz sat gazing up at Jethro with unconcealed humor and Jethro continued to wave his arms wildly to make his point. The miners clustered around the pair seemed to find the situation as amusing as Griz did, and that fact whipped Jethro to greater heights of fury.

Omaha could only catch a word or two here and there when voices were particularly loud, but he gathered from it that this was Sunday, the Sabbath, and a horse race was scheduled for later that day. The fact did not seem to be sitting too well with Jethro, especially in view of the behavior that was already taking place in the camp in the early morning hours, when, in his opinion, there should have been worship.

It was equally plain that no one planned to cancel the race on some self-proclaimed preacher's account, and Jethro's anger continued to grow until he puffed himself up like a fighting cock and said that he too would ride in the race. With his usual fiery delivery he claimed he would win the race with ease with the Lord's help and take their money from them for their sinfulness. A large guffaw rose at one end of the saloon at his statement and rolled through it, growing louder as it traveled until Jethro sought his

169

exit with strained dignity.

Ducking his head to keep Jethro from seeing his face as he passed through the doors, Omaha came face to face with the man who occupied the table he had, without invitation, seated himself at. Peering at Omaha through narrow slits of eyes that were watering on either side of a red nose, he looked at him with great seriousness.

'There's gonna be Injun trouble here soon, son.' He imparted the information as if it were gospel. 'Real soon.'

The old man in buckskins was obviously drunk, and Griz was free now, so Omaha made a move to rise, pondering how Griz had gone ahead and made arrangements for the race without knowing Emily's whereabouts, when a gnarled hand reached out and held him with surprising force in his seat.

'Trouble,' the old scout said with a serious nod of his head just before he tossed another drink down. 'Take my word, son, I seen it a'comin',' he said with a dry chuckle. 'Followed them Injuns all the way through the Goosenecks east of here, I did,' he said thickly, 'and I know they ain't up to no good.' He shook his head slowly. 'Noooo good.'

Omaha knew the same thing, but for different reasons, if the Indians the old drunk was muttering about were the same band the old chief who had talked to the slimy gunslick behind Belle's sporting house headed up.

'Nobody around these parts believes me, son,' the old scout persisted through his drunkenness, 'but I been scouting these mountains and valleys since before most of 'em was born and I know trouble when I see it mounted up and ridin'.'

'I believe you,' Omaha assured him, trying to break free from his steely grasp without resorting to definite action. Then he paused, looking at the man more closely. Something clicked, a tinkling bell of memory went off in his brain.

The Goosenecks, the old scout had said something about the Goosenecks. The memory of Omaha's flight, both harrowing and exhilarating, through the tightly twisting Goosenecks flashed through his mind. A band of Indians had been in the canyons, and a lone scout. The man riding hunched in his saddle, dressed in buckskins with almost white hair blowing beneath a floppy leather hat. In his careening flight Omaha had not seen the lone man clearly, but he was sure this was the man. There could hardly be another in the same time span.

'Where are the Indians camped?' Omaha asked.

The old scout peered at Omaha through his alcoholic haze as his eyes again narrowed to slits in his leathery face. 'They're camped southwest of here. Couple a' miles.' The old scout imparted the information almost grudgingly. 'They're Sioux,' he said behind a suppressed hiccup. 'Hope you ain't plannin' on takin' 'em on your own self.

'Now, the two a' us together,' the old scout added, perking up. 'Well...'

'I'm not planning on fighting them,' Omaha said quickly. 'I'm planning on stopping them.'

'Same thing,' the old scout said flatly.

'Not when you're half Sioux yourself,' Omaha said evenly, and pressed the argument no further as he rose from his chair and left the old scout to his bottle.

Griz's face broke into a broad smile that stretched across his stained teeth so wide it looked as if it should hurt when he saw Omaha approaching, elbowing his way through the bulky bodies that were pressed into the room so tightly they resembled canned sardines.

'Well!' Griz yelled above the crowd. 'Knew you would find me here sooner or later.' His red-brown hair gleamed dully beneath the overhead lamps, and his eyes, usually sharp and hawklike, glittered with genuine pleasure at seeing Omaha. In the early hours of dawn before he had hit Kingman's camp, he had not been all that sure he *would* see him again.

He and Otto had come into Kingman's camp under a head of steam Griz had had building since he had found the evidence of the skirmish. As luck would have it, the first person Griz laid eyes on when he came into the camp was Mac, the proprietor of the bawdy house where Cinnamon had taken refuge and been taken beneath Belle's wing. Being an old acquaintance, Mac had immediately informed him of Emily's whereabouts and the safety of the girl riding her and the fact that she had been seen taking in a somewhat oddly dressed companion for the night. Griz's steam had evaporated in a mist. Everything, then, had been settled. With a new sense of security, Griz had retired to the nearest saloon to wait for Omaha to show up. While he had been waiting, idling away the hours, he had just naturally taken the opportunity to set up a horse race for that afternoon. At that point it had never occurred to him that he would not tie up with Omaha again before then.

'You set up a race already?' Omaha breathed as he slid into the chair opposite Griz, throwing a glance beneath the big man's chair, where Ezra lay curled up in a tight ball, not so much as a tuft of fur sticking out beyond the chair's four corners of protection. Omaha grinned. 'It *was* Ezra I heard howling earlier.'

Griz returned the grin. 'Yup, sure was.

Ezra gets nervous when we get in around folks, 'specially a lot of folks like here.' He paused, breaking off his remark, then nodded in the affirmative to Omaha's question of greeting. 'I got us a race set up right quick,' Griz admitted with pride. 'Didn't you hear that righteous discussion all us sinful gambling men were having with that black-coated traveling preacher?' Griz gave a great rumbling laugh as Otto appeared from the fringes of the crowd and joined them at the table, a beer clenched in one hand. 'Why, we're so sinful, he's gonna ride in the race with us.' Griz laughed again at the absurdity of it.

'I saw him,' Omaha said, 'and he's not just some ordinary preacher passing through. He's Cinnamon's stepbrother and he's about as determined as any man can be that he's going to take her back and marry her if he can get his hands on her again.'

'She been runnin' away from him all this time?' Griz asked. 'He put them bullets in your campfire and damn near killed us all?'

Omaha nodded and related the rest of the story since he had last seen Griz and Otto down by the riverbank where Jethro had pulled Cinnamon from the water and disappeared into the trees with her across his saddle.

Griz frowned when he came to the part where Cinnamon had lit out on Emily and

174

Omaha had followed on Jethro's horse. Otto shook his head in disbelief and kept muttering softly to himself, 'Poor little Liebschen.'

When Omaha finished, Griz grunted and poured himself another drink from a bottle that sat in the middle of their table. 'No wonder that little gal is plumb loco,' Griz remarked without inflection. 'Never did see a little filly as skittish as her.'

Omaha shot him a sideways glance that he either did not see or chose not to. And then he started to tell Griz and Otto what he had overheard beside the corral out behind the wood and canvas whorehouse and gambling establishment.

'None a' our affair,' Griz broke in as Omaha went on, 'and we'll take care a' old Jethro in the race this afternoon. That's all you got to think about.' In truth there was much more to these races than running. Griz glanced around for the barkeep, caught his eye, and bellowed across the room, 'Bring us another bottle—and another beer,' noting the almost empty mug in Otto's hand.

Otto, though, was a different matter. His English was not yet perfect, but he had picked up plenty, and there was little that now escaped his understanding. Omaha's news was distressing. The supply train approaching Kingman's camp could only be the one he had been tied in with before his mare had foaled. He had arrived in town sooner because of Griz's shortcuts through the mountains. The men on the supply train were old friends. He could not allow what Omaha predicted to happen without being a part of trying to stop it. If Omaha was willing to make the effort, then he was too.

The barkeep Griz had summoned paused beside their table, his round flabby face screwed up as if he smelled something bad. 'Can't serve Injuns,' he said flatly, his eyes fixed on Omaha and his strange attire and obvious Indian heritage.

'Hell,' Griz roared irritably, 'he's as white as me!' He paused, glancing sideways at Omaha and his obvious Indian features. 'Well, anyway, at least half as white as me!' he ended, thumping his chest. 'Now, you go on ahead and pour that white half a drink before I break your leg,' Griz advised pleasantly.

Few were inclined to buck Griz when he gave a direct order, and the barkeep was no exception. With a grunt of irritation, he poured a drink into the glass in front of Omaha and left the bottle, taking the empty one with him when he left.

'That's him, that's the man I saw by the corral talking to the Sioux chief,' Omaha abruptly directed their mixed attention to the saloon's batwings. 'Do you know him?'

It seemed as if nearly every eye in the place

had turned in the direction of the door when the stranger dressed in black stepped through it, his thin, long-fingered hand hovering near his six-gun, his angular face showing no emotion, and his black hooded eyes hiding all that lurked in their depths.

Otto looked interested, but Griz's face puffed out as he blew his breath out in a short burst. 'Chrrrrist, boy.' Griz's green eyes went hard, his voice gruff and low. 'Where you been living, in a hole? That there's Haqihana. Meanest damn breed to ever come up the pike. Pardon me, son,' he said as if catching the insult he had inadvertently thrown at Omaha, 'but I ain't comparin' you to him, not for a minute! That'n,' he went on quickly, 'went bad a long time ago. He ain't nothin' but pure poison. And what's worse is he's got real talent. I doubt there's a man alive can outdraw him in a fair fight or an unfair one, which is what he's best at.'

Keeping his voice in a gruff whisper so he would not draw the attention of the object of their discussion, Griz went on as the bartender moved to serve Haqihana with none of the objections he had raised to Omaha's presence. 'His pa was Arapaho, his ma, white, captured when things first started kicking up in those parts. Haqihana ain't got no love for no man. Last count, he'd killed twenty-six men, and that don't include those they ain't counted! Don't you go messin' with him,' Griz admonished Omaha in an almost fatherly tone. 'Just 'cause you're wearing that six-gun I give you don't mean you're a match for him.'

Omaha stared at him as Haqihana made himself comfortable at a table where the occupants had suddenly, as a group, gotten up and moved to the bar.

Haqihana. The name meant something. Omaha knew when Griz had said it that he had heard it before. Maybe it was back when his tribe had been camped near El Capitan. Haqihana. He knew all Griz had said about him was true, and his eyes slid past him, then back again to meet the icy gaze of his counterpart. Hearing about the man's background did not change the fact that Omaha, deep inside, knew he had to stop him. Somehow.

CHAPTER THIRTEEN

Omaha stared hard at Griz. He did not think there would be any way to sway the older man's opinion, but it did not matter. He would do what he had to do. It was probably better in most ways that Griz was not too eager to take a part in it. More than once, in the past, his help had almost been their undoing. And, the way Omaha felt, knowing the many problems between the Sioux people and the whites, it was more his job than Griz's anyway. After all, he had been the one who had overheard the conversation that took place behind Mac's between the old chief and the half-breed renegade who called himself Haqihana. The only other person in camp who had the slightest inkling of the trouble brewing was the old drunken scout who still occupied a table near the door.

'I will help you,' Otto spoke up, breaking the long silence between Omaha and Griz. His sparkling blue eyes were fixed on the object of Omaha's attention, Haqihana. 'Ja,' he said with sincerity, 'I will help you to stop this, my friend.'

Startled by his proclamation, Omaha quickly glanced sideways at Otto, and one look told him the heavyset Dutchman meant every word he said. The realization took Omaha aback, for he had already begun to formulate plans of his own, and they had included no one but himself, and, of course, his wings. Fully armed, he planned to launch himself from the highest point in Kingman's camp, and with surprise on his side, bear down on the attackers and drive them off. The plan and course of action were simple, and Omaha had little doubt that it would work, while at the same time giving a sterling showcase for the immense practicality of his wings. Once and for all it would prove their usefulness. Flying, he was convinced, would one day be a way of life just as riding a horse was as permanent as the grasses that grew on the prairies. Soon, others would be airborne just as he had been, and would be again. They would glide on outstretched wings as he had, using the thongs Otto and Cinnamon had designed for quick release and even for maneuvering, a problem which had yet to be overcome completely.

'Good,' Omaha said without enthusiasm, not knowing what he could do with Otto's assistance, but knowing it would not be wise to turn down any offer of help. Maybe the cobbler could help him get his wings up to the launch point once he established where that was going to be. And that, of course, depended on the direction of the pack train's approach as well as the angle of attack the old chief and his warriors would decide on. Omaha felt a twinge somewhere down deep. There would be mayhem and chaos if his plan did not work. On both sides. Both now, and later. Omaha cast a dark glance in Haqihana's direction and was again met by the penetrating gaze of his unmoving, snakelike black eyes. Fixed and steady, they remained fastened on Omaha. It was almost as if the other man could somehow read his thoughts and was at the same time laughing at him.

Shaking off the feeling with a shrug, Omaha matched Haqihana stare for stare until the other man's dark eyes flicked elsewhere, still hooded, still sliding around the room with an unmistakable snakelike quality.

Griz gave Omaha a sullen, forbidding look, then shifted his gaze back to the other half-breed, his green eyes sharp and piercing as they caught and held Haqihana, uncaring, in their grip. He grunted something under his breath that could not have been pleasant, then turned to face Omaha.

'Hope to hell you don't cross swords with that one until after the race this afternoon. Can't afford to lose you 'til then.'

Omaha ignored the remark and turned to Otto. 'Maybe you better take that horse of yours and ride out a ways. See if you can see any sign of that pack train coming in.'

Clasping his hat in his hand Otto nodded eagerly, glad to have something he could do. Almost jumping up out of his chair, he started for the door while Griz swung his gaze once more in the direction of Haqihana, and what he saw there made his blood run cold. A stillness settled on that end of the room and a cold smile curled the half-breed's lips. Closer to their own table, Griz suddenly spotted the reason. There was some damn fool almost anywhere a man

181

went who would be stupid enough to want to try his luck against a gunman with the reputation Haqihana toted along with him wherever he went. Kingman's camp was no exception, and half the trash in the country was condensed down into that small hollow in the mountains the camp occupied. Spraddle-legged, a man stood before Haqihana, both his sobriety and his intelligence severely lacking as far as Griz was concerned, and he was calling him out, just as bold as brass. No one had seemed to take much notice of the situation yet, save Haqihana, the sneering stranger, and Griz, who did not like the approaching stranger's proximity to his table. If there was going to be lead flying, and there seemed now almost no chance of avoiding it, Griz Tanner was a man with enough sense to put plenty of distance between himself and the source.

'Gun trouble.' Griz leaned over to Omaha, uttering the two words just as calm as you please before he slid the rest of the way to the floor, dipping rapidly below Omaha's startled gaze.

Omaha jerked around as if he had been slapped, his eyes again focusing on Haqihana an instant before the guns came out. Haqihana never stirred from where he sat. Almost instantly his gun was out, while the stupid stranger was still reaching for his. In a heartbeat Omaha realized what Griz had known. His position at the table was almost dead between the fighting pair. He heard Cinnamon scream. Cinnamon? Then there was a mad scrambling of paws beneath his chair and Omaha felt himself going over sideways, chair and all, as six-guns cracked sharply in the close confines of the crowded saloon.

The explosion of action took Omaha almost entirely by surprise as it erupted around him, and for an instant, his world already in a spin as his chair made for the floor by the most indirect route, it made no more sense to Omaha than a scrambled egg. Deep-throated grunts sounded all around him as others dove unceremoniously for cover and the scramble of paws continued beneath his chair as Ezra, whining softly in his terror of guns, darted through the set of the chair's legs and into the open. The smoke had not cleared, and the guns had cracked more than once, though Omaha had not kept count, and he heard Cinnamon scream again though his mind could still not accept her presence when he had specifically told her not to be there. Griz swore, yelling in Ezra's direction, and Omaha hit the floorboards with a clatter and a thump that felt like he was going to go right on through. Abruptly, the room fell into a deep silence. Omaha found himself sprawled on the floor beside the idiot who had opened the ball and

Ezra, who lay in an odd posture, breathing in rapid little gasps and whimpering softly as his tail thumped weakly against the floorboards beside Omaha's face.

One glance at the sneering stranger told the whole story as Omaha rolled with a wince to his knees. He would not be calling out another gunslick again, Haqihana had ended that permanently with a piece of lead through the heart. Omaha bent over the wounded coyote as Griz scrambled up behind him, reaching out a rough, gnarled hand to the softly whining animal. In view of the coyote's timidity where guns were concerned, it was obvious that Ezra's actions had been far from purposeful. However, accidentally or not, the fact remained fixed in Omaha's brain that the animal had saved his life when he had overturned the chair. Blood was staining the coyote's thick gray fur as well as the floorboards beneath him and Omaha knew that poor, timid, gun-shy Ezra was dying. Something caught in Omaha's throat as he watched Griz, tears filling his eyes but not spilling over, reach out to comfort his old friend. Maybe in the eyes of most people Ezra had been a no-account coyote, but to Griz he had been a real friend. Suddenly, Cinnamon appeared from out of nowhere with the camp's combination horse and people doctor in tow.

'Do something!' Cinnamon demanded,

pushing the doc forward.

Obediently, as long as this was going to be a cash call as Miss Cinnamon had promised him it would be, the doc bent over the bleeding animal. But, even as he began to pack the wound, Ezra nuzzled closer to Griz's hand, gave a long, low sigh, and slipped quietly away.

'Oh,' Griz said softly with a catch in his throat, 'hell.'

A sad look on his face, the doc slowly stood up, and finally turned his attention to the stranger who had started the melee and whom everyone had already known to be past needing any care. The matter closed, the room went back to drinking and gambling with only slightly subdued gusto.

The dead stranger caused no shedding of tears, and was hardly given a backward glance. But Cinnamon, dressed in her red spangled dress, wept openly for Ezra, the tears running in a torrent down her apple cheeks and her blue eyes awash with new ones, yet to be shed.

Haqihana still sat where he had seated himself when he had come in, calmly sipping his drink as if nothing had happened within the past few minutes that concerned him in the least. His gun was back in his holster and his hooded eyes remained fixed on Omaha, Griz, and Cinnamon, staring steadily at them over the rim of his glass as the poignant drama unfolded before him. He had not seen the animal pass before his gun, but if he had, he would not have cared. One less coyote in the world was nothing to sniffle over as the girl, attractive for all her red swollen eyes, red nose, and tear-streaked cheeks, did now. In a slow, appraising caress his eyes moved up and down her though she took no notice of it, being too wound up in her own thoughts. His face, cold and unmoved, he gazed at her. She was interesting, and the way she was dressed made it a limited number of places where she might be later. And he knew he had seen her before at Mac's. He would find her later, if he was not busy elsewhere.

Otto, barely out the door, had turned when he heard the shots. Hurrying back inside he saw it was already too late. Nothing could be done to change what had happened. And with sadness he watched as Griz scooped Ezra up into his arms. A chilled new silence spread through the room as Griz stood there, Ezra in his arms, and he and Haqihana locked eyes across the room. Griz's gaze was hot and murderous. As always Haqihana remained unchanged, his eyes merely returning Griz's stare. In fact an onlooker might have said a touch of amusement was in the depths of the hooded black eyes. Amusement because he knew for all of Griz Tanner's commanding manner, huge bulk, and unquestioned strength, he would not dare to challenge him where he sat. Only the stupid, inexperienced, or overly cocky tried that, and Grizzly Tanner was none of those. So, like any reasonably intelligent man wanting to preserve his own hide, he would take his loss and that would be the end of it in this room.

Omaha, though, read something different in Griz's look. Without a gesture, without a word being said, he knew he had gained himself a new partner in his determined drive to stop the attack on the pack train. Griz Tanner was a devious man. He would take his revenge in his own way, and in Haqihana's case that could not be out in the open, face to face. Omaha was not sure how pleased he was with the new situation; only time would tell. Only minutes before, he had talked himself into being almost happy that Griz would not be lending a hand in his crusade. Now the plans were again being complicated. Actually there were no definite plans, and Omaha was beginning to wish he could take his wings to the nearest mountaintop, jump off, and fly away, but he knew he could not. Only one course was left open to him, and that was to grit his teeth and follow through with what he had begun, even if that meant trying to keep track of Cinnamon on one hand, and running a good horse race on the other. With Griz in the state he was, he wondered about the race and then he remembered Cinnamon.

His gaze shot from corner to corner of the crowded saloon like a ricochet, coming to rest on her at last where she stood not far from the door. Omaha could not think of a better place to find her. With long, quickening strides, he slid up to her, placed an arm possessively about her slim, white, and very exposed shoulders, and started to guide her neatly out the door.

They had not taken two steps in that direction behind Griz and Otto's exit when the batwings flew open before them and Jethro strode into the room, coattails flying. Before he even got through the door, his mouth was open, launching into one of his loud and lengthy sermons on the evils that lurked in a place with the character of Kingman's camp. The news of the shooting had traveled to his ears with amazing speed, or perhaps he had heard the gunshots himself somewhere out on the street and followed them to their source.

With unerring judgment, Omaha pressed Cinnamon's face close against his chest, pulled his hat brim low, and bent his head down over hers as they passed Jethro, preoccupied with the many sins of men, and eased right out the door without drawing his attention. Only Omaha's hand over her mouth had kept Cinnamon from squeaking her surprise when Jethro had suddenly appeared, and, once outside, she breathed a long sigh of relief. Omaha glanced anxiously over his shoulder to see if they had been followed from the saloon, but no one passed through the doors behind them. And because Omaha did not see the pair of eyes gazing fixedly at them out of the saloon window, he joined Cinnamon in her relief that they had slipped past Jethro so easily. He had not enjoyed the moment when they had passed within handshaking distance of Jethro and he had felt Cinnamon tense as he had held her close to him.

Without thinking, Omaha clasped Cinnamon's hand in his as he hastened after Griz and Otto, dragging her along behind him at a skipping run. He had seen them disappear around the corner in front of them, and he knew where they had to be headed. Griz would want to bury Ezra, and Otto was plainly planning on lending a hand. Omaha could feel for Griz's sorrow, but he had to know about the race, and Otto had to be up on his horse scouting for some sign of the supply train's approach or everything they hoped to accomplish would be lost. Haqihana and the Indians would hit it with nothing to stop them, and the valley below Kingman's camp would run red with blood. From Omaha's experience he had found little mercy on either side. And once the

Indians started drinking and clashed with the already besotted souls of Kingman's camp, the whole thing could turn into a massacre of one side or the other. Which one would emerge victorious was something Omaha believed open to debate. He was going to have to give Griz a hand himself and send Otto out to do what he had started to leave the saloon to do in the first place. When Omaha and Cinnamon caught up with them, Griz had already sunk a shovel into the soft earth, and Otto had respectfully wrapped Ezra's body in a tarp.

'Griz,' Omaha began tentatively. 'Griz, if we're going to pay back Haqihana for what he did, if we're going to stop him and the renegades from hitting that supply train, we need Otto out in the hills keeping an eye out for them.' Omaha made the statement of plain fact as gently as he could, knowing the friendship that had blossomed between the two men. 'I would go myself, but if the race is still on...'

''Course it's still on,' Griz snapped irritably. 'Can't back out 'cause this here happened. 'Sides, Ezra would want me to go ahead like nothin' happened.'

'I'll give you a hand,' Omaha offered, dropping Cinnamon's cool hand from where it had rested, comforted, in his own, and picked up the second shovel to dig.

Griz grunted and nodded shortly to Otto.

'You better get a move on if you're still figurin' on giving them old friends of yours some help.' Griz's commanding manner seemingly gave Otto little choice in the matter.

Quick to accept the logic in what they were saying, Otto turned and retraced his steps toward the front of the saloon, where he had left his horse. Pausing in mid-stride, he glanced back over his shoulder at Cinnamon and while he had not yet said anything about her strange change in wearing apparel since their arrival in Kingman's camp, Cinnamon feared that this would be the time.

Instead, he gave a weak half-smile like a small boy asking a favor and said, 'You will look after little one for me?'

Cinnamon nodded, knowing he meant the foal, who had been sharing the hitching rack with his mother.

Otto turned on his heel with a snap, and disappeared around the corner.

Ezra's burial was swift and quiet, Griz digging with the effort of two men, and Omaha pitching in. Griz claimed it was the way Ezra would have wanted it, and both men knew they had little time to spare. The time for the race had been set for the early afternoon hours and that time was rapidly drawing near. The whole camp was in an uproar over it, it would not be wise to be late.

Cinnamon retrieved Otto's foal from where it had been standing by the hitching rack pitifully whinnying for its missing mother and put him in the corral with Emily, who immediately started to mother him. The colt would be disappointed soon when Emily was saddled up for the race, but for the moment he was content. And, for the moment, all they could do was wait.

CHAPTER FOURTEEN

The sun blazed down from a crystal blue sky with not even a cotton ball of a cloud to break the endless blue expanse. Pleasantly warm, there was only the faintest suggestion of a breeze starting to rise out of the southwest. The valley sprawled at the feet of Kingman's camp teemed with the camp's residents who had turned out for the race in a jovial, boisterous mood almost as if a circus had just come to town. Bets were being laid down thick and fast, with no single horse seeming to come out the favorite, which was certainly to Griz's liking. His Emily was hardly ever favored to lead the pack, and that opened up many other avenues of profit making. He was able to place many private bets on the side on top of covering almost any comers foolhardy enough to be betting against his Emily.

Omaha Jones stood beside Emily where she was already saddled at the starting line, dancing lightly on her toes in anticipation of what she knew so well. Her soft brown eyes bright and alert, she was more than ready. She was eager, and her ears flicked forward as she tugged continually at the reins Omaha held firmly in his hand. There was no doubt in Omaha's mind that she would win and he watched her toss her head so that her silken mane glistened in the bright sunlight.

Griz, lost in the crowd somewhere, was still taking and making bets and the race was going to start at any minute, but at the moment only three things held Omaha's attention. One of them was Haqihana where he lounged about the fringes of the rippling, ever moving crowd, and the constant, almost casual attention he seemed to pay to the clear blue sky out toward the southeastern horizon. He was watching for something, smoke signals maybe. Another was Otto's prolonged absence. There had been no sign or signal from him for hours and Omaha was beginning to get nervous about what it could mean. There was the probability that he had simply not located the approaching pack train of supplies, that it might not show up for days yet, but somehow he knew that was not what it was. Still, Haqihana was too calm, too unconcerned where he drifted along on the fringes of the crowd, his hooded gaze continually flickering over the tops of the people between them to lock eyes with Omaha. Whether it was accidental or intentional, Omaha was acutely aware of it. Even more so than the cold, fish-eyed glare he had been receiving from Jethro Clayton ever since he had arrived with his horse and recognized Omaha with Emily.

Other members of the camp gathered around with the horses they had entered, turning the starting line into a milling mass of humanity and horseflesh, but still Omaha was aware of that cold glare focused on his back. It was just as well, to Omaha's way of thinking. The more Jethro concentrated on him, the less likelihood there would be of his spotting Cinnamon in the crowd that pressed in around them. She was there; Omaha had caught an occasional glimpse of her, and it would not have been hard for Jethro to do so as well if he had taken his eyes off Omaha for a few seconds to look.

The idea of Cinnamon coming down to watch the race had not set too well with Omaha; he had wanted her to keep well out of sight. Cinnamon, though, had protested that during the race Jethro would not have time to do anything even if he did see her, which she would make sure he did not do in the first place. It was nice, Omaha reflected, to have that kind of faith.

The route for the race had been clearly defined. It swept through the lush green valley running almost due east away from the camp, then swung abruptly north through some low hills, angling back past the camp. Then east again for a short burst past some of the mines that were responsible for Kingman's camp's creation, down through the camp itself, and back out into the valley, ending up back at the starting line. Ten other horses had been entered in the race besides Emily and Jethro's horse. And the only rule governing their behavior during the race was the complete absence of any rules at all. It was every man for himself, no holds barred, and it would be a hell-for-leather run start to finish. There was nothing polished about camp town races and while Omaha had never been in one himself, he was the first to acknowledge that fact. One look at the burly miners and greasy gamblers entered was enough to convince even the most trusting that there would be a lot more to this race than a fast horse. It was something Griz had neglected to mention when they had formed their partnership.

'Riders up!' someone shouted with authority, and Griz almost instantly reappeared at Omaha's side as if he had never been gone.

'Just turn her loose,' Griz whispered to

Omaha as Omaha swung into the saddle without touching a stirrup. 'She knows what she's doin'. Just get her in front and keep her there. We got us a real good stake.'

Omaha nodded, not knowing how hard that feat would be to accomplish with such as what he was going to be riding the race against. Emily was the fastest, there was no doubt about that, but that was not all that would count in this race. It would be more like a brawl on horseback, and though Griz was certainly right in wanting to get Emily clear of it as soon as possible, the problem lay in the fact that Emily was not a fast starter. She seemed to build up speed as she ran, but it would take her quite a few strides to get her rhythm, and by then they could have trouble. There would be no way to anticipate it, and Omaha knew he would have to take care of each situation as it came up. To make matters worse, he had no history of past races to go by.

As the others stepped, jumped, or swung into their saddles, Omaha gave one last quick glance around for Cinnamon. The gesture was almost reflex as he had been doing it so often. With a start he realized he could not spot her anywhere in the vicinity of where she had been previously.

'Get ready!' The starter barked the order sharply to let his voice be heard above the din of the surrounding crowd where it was packed behind the starting line.

Omaha's eyes slid over the crowd with a sudden feeling of apprehension. Jethro was mounted a couple of horses down the line, his piercing brown eyes still fastened on Omaha more than on what lay before them. He had never been out of Omaha's sight, so he could have done nothing. Cinnamon had promised to stay near Griz during the race, but something had obviously changed her mind. Omaha frowned darkly. She was a headstrong girl, given to doing anything she damned pleased. Almost anything could have drawn her off, and Omaha swore under his breath that he was going to strangle her once the race was over, until he realized with a start that Haqihana was also missing. Where was he?!

A rising feeling of panic welled up inside Omaha as Griz stepped well back and the starting gun was raised to be fired. Then he spotted Cinnamon. And, separated by a considerable crowd of people, but not more than a dozen strides behind her, was Haqihana.

At that same instant, the starting gun was fired. The ear-shocking crack of it echoed down the length of the valley, seeming to fade off in the same direction as the running horses, who launched themselves in a headlong dive at the starter's signal. With a wild display of flailing arms, legs, and bellowed oaths, the riders were away from the starting line and pounding feverishly across the valley's green turf.

For a moment, Omaha tried to pull Emily up short as the gun had sounded in his hears, but Emily was well seasoned and wearing the bridle Griz had designed for her tender mouth and supposedly delicate nature. It left her almost totally uncontrolled, save for direction, in which she was willing to oblige as long as it took her along with the others pounding on either side of her. After a moment, sensibly, Omaha gave up trying to fight her as her strides continued to lengthen and her nose reached out for the empty space ahead of her. The sooner he took her full circle, the sooner he would be able to find out what was going on back in camp. Cinnamon had proved long before that she was a resourceful girl, she would have to handle matters until then.

Intent upon watching the riders and the excitement that surrounded them, Cinnamon had craned her neck to see around and over those in front of her. A couple of times she had caught Omaha's eye while Griz had been busy taking and placing bets on the race. She had wondered about Otto. There had been no sign of him since he had left hours before to scout the countryside to catch sight of his erstwhile cohorts of the trail, the men bringing in the supply train. Her attention had been divided between searching the horizon for some sign of Otto's approach, and keeping an eye on Omaha as the race readied itself to begin, when suddenly she was aware of a presence near her. It was not just another person; they were packed around her like sardines in a can, each craning to get a better look at the proceedings. It was more like an icy chill. Turning, yet almost half afraid to turn, Cinnamon almost turned into Haqihana's arms. In fact, she would have had he not been standing there calmly regarding her, his arms folded over his chest.

With a start Cinnamon jumped back, bumping into a miner, who took no notice of her at all. After the display she had inadvertently witnessed in the saloon earlier she feared this man, even beyond all reason. It was not even the fact that he had killed a man in a gunfight—she had seen men killed before. It was the way he had done it. The cold uncaring efficiency with which he had dispatched him.

His black eyes glittering, Haqihana watched her closely, a tight smile tugging at the corners of his mouth. Cinnamon pulled herself together and managed to stand straight and tall before him, returning his gaze with hers of wide, blue-eyed innocence.

'I could use some companionship,' Haqihana addressed her quietly, his voice low, with an odd caressing quality, his words heavy with a deeper meaning.

Cinnamon gulped, the sound audible only to herself. Then, somehow, she managed a pinched little smile. 'I can't,' she answered, realizing how stupid her words were as she said them. 'I came down here to watch the race,' she ended lamely as the riders took to their saddles.

'It's not important,' Haqihana returned, stepping close beside her, letting his hard eyes run across her soft white shoulders where the red spangled dress covered them not at all.

Feeling her hair brush across her shoulder as it was swept back in the rising breeze, Cinnamon fell back another half step, but he followed her, laying a long-fingered hand on her bare shoulder, his grip tightening as their eyes locked.

'Where're you trying to slip away to?' Haqihana questioned lightly. 'There's nowhere to go.' His words were clear, their meaning obvious.

'I ... I can't help you,' Cinnamon stammered, uncertain how to word her refusal. 'I ... I'm engaged,' she lied quickly.

'You sure are,' Haqihana replied laconically. 'I'm engaging your services right now.'

'No!' Cinnamon exclaimed before she could contain it. Haqihana's eyebrow shot up in a questioning arch. 'No,' Cinnamon said more softly, getting a fresh hold on herself. 'I'm engaged to be married. I'm in a family way,' she said quickly, falling back on an old lie that had saved her bacon before as she tried to squirm free of his grasp. 'The father of my child is riding in the race,' she embroidered the story further as she continued to twist and turn, finally squirming free of Haqihana's less than gentle grasp.

He smiled like a cat eyeing a mouse it was using for a plaything before the kill. His black eyes took on their hooded appearance as they moved slowly up and down Cinnamon's hard, slender form, appraising her as if she stood before him unclothed. Cinnamon could read nothing in the depths of his diamond-hard eyes.

'I hope the child is not due soon,' Haqihana commented with wry humor.

'Well...' Cinnamon began.

'So,' Haqihana cut her off. 'You want to play games.' He grinned, his eyes again glittering like chips of glass, and Cinnamon knew the situation had gotten suddenly worse. 'I like to play games with my women,' he said softly, and Cinnamon could almost feel him getting ready to reach for her.

With a gasp, she eluded him, ducking under a heavyset miner's arm and squirming into the next packed row of people before

Haqihana realized what had happened. Being small, Cinnamon slid and squirmed, poked and pinched her way through the crowd, for the moment gaining ground on Haqihana, who, she saw when she glanced over her shoulder behind her, was following, but at a slower pace than she was managing. Once she was free of the crowd, though, she knew it would be no contest. He would regain the lost ground rapidly, and then she would be out in the open. The entire camp would be watching the race and none of them save Griz, Omaha, or Otto would have the nerve to do anything even if they knew of her peril. Behind her, Cinnamon heard the starter yell for the riders to get ready, and a few seconds later, the starting gun sounded. Cinnamon did not turn back. Omaha had warned her about going down to watch the race, and now he would not even know anything had happened until he got back and could not find any sign of her. She was on her own again, a condition she seemed to find herself in most of the time.

Abruptly, the empty space that had stretched out before Emily was blocked, and Omaha had his hands full. Emily's strides shortened with jarring swiftness and she almost buck-jumped as Omaha tried to keep her from running right up the tail of the horse that had swung in front of them. It was early in the race and Emily had just begun to stretch out when one of the riders from the left of them had pulled the fancy maneuver. Apparently he had seen Emily starting to pull away slowly and nursed an extra burst of speed from his horse, slipping into Omaha's side vision like a shot out of a gun.

From the other side there approached a rider who was carrying a long stick, its obvious use being to encourage his mount to greater efforts, its not so obvious use being to poke, slap, or trip the other horses, causing them to shy or fall and pile up the rest of the riders pounding down on them from behind. Omaha kept a wary eye on him, and to that point had managed to keep Emily clear of his vicinity, but now the stick wielder was swerving his mount in their direction, a gleam in his eye. Before the race, Griz had been right, there were not many who put much stock in Emily's abilities, but once out and running those riding against her were no fools. Within only a few strides it became painfully clear which horse was the real threat. If Emily got clear of the pack, there would be no stopping her, and the other riders were as well aware of that fact now as Omaha, and they were intent on stopping her.

That, though, did not mean that they were going after her as a mob, there were still plenty of battles going on among themselves to keep most of the riders occupied. One pair to the rear, off Emily's right flank, were exchanging blows as their horses ran at top speed, each trying, so far without success, to unseat the other. Another duo, apparently riding in the race as partners, had ridden down a third, tried to unseat him, somehow got their spurs tangled, and all three had gone down in a tangle of arms, legs, and wildly kicking horses, considerably thinning the field of horses that remained to finish the race.

Emily, used to being a front runner, was considerably irritated by the position she now found herself in. Continually, she tossed her fine head, snorting loudly, and breaking stride often at her enforced erratic pace. And there was nothing about the approach of the rider with the stick that pleased her. Omaha could feel the contained power beneath his knees, he could feel the impatience building in the animal, and he knew he would have to do something about their position soon, but for the moment they were completely boxed. Omaha glanced over his shoulder. They were boxed from three sides, but not from behind. The next rider was a good three or four horse lengths behind. Though people were in clumps all along the length of the race course, Omaha was not even aware of them. He thought only of his horse, and what they had to do.

There was no choice. If Omaha remained

where he was, they could very well finish the race just as they were running now, the horse that had cut him off in front, and one to either side, or, worse, the ambitious rider wielding the stick could bring Emily down. Omaha ground his teeth as they swept off the broad green expanse of the valley and entered the hills to the north. They had to go around the trio, somehow.

Taking a deep breath as the rider with the stick closed in on them brandishing it with wild, enthusiastic cowboy yelps as he neared his goal, Omaha spoke to Emily, hoping he would not have to fight her, and gave a sharp tug on the reins. To his surprise, Emily almost locked her legs, giving Omaha a jarring ride that nearly threw him from the saddle over her head as he pulled her sharply to one side, and the closest rider behind bore down on them, unable to stop. Touching his heels to her flanks, Omaha urged her forward at an angle that would take her behind the plunging rider with the maniac's gleam and the heavy stick, and slip narrowly in front of the rider bearing uncontrollably down on them from behind. The dust whipped up in a swirl around them, powdering over Omaha's eyeballs as he felt Emily's hoofs dig into the hard-packed earth, and her hindquarters gather beneath her for a magnificent leap that took them forward into a headlong run. One jump and she was nearly alongside the stick-wielding rider, another and she was going past before he had a chance to put it to use. Panicked at the near collision, the horse in the rear shied sideways, throwing his rider into the dust. Then, suddenly, there was open country before them and Emily was running free. Omaha could feel the power beneath her sleek hide, feel the rhythmic gathering of muscles as she stretched out, and her strides again began to lengthen.

On the far side of the packed horses, Omaha saw something else. With a lordly bellow and sharp clip to the jaw of a man who had been trying to drag him from the saddle, Jethro Clayton also broke clear, and the thing was finally turning into a horse race. That was, unless Jethro had other ideas.

Jethro's horse was a sturdy animal and he was still running well, but half of the course still lay ahead of them. Dust was rising around them in thick clouds now that they had left the lush green of the valley behind, and steep hills rolled to either side and in front of them as they pressed on, the horses fearlessly taking to them like mountain goats. The field of runners had been sharply reduced by the first mad run across the valley floor, and now the pace was beginning to tell on some of the other animals, but not Emily. She took the hills head on, up and over, her hoofs clattering rhythmically against stone as they slid from beneath her swiftly flying feet, rolling down the hillside in her wake. Some of the other riders, including Jethro, swung their mounts around some of the hills, saving their horses for the run that yet lay ahead. Omaha tried it with Emily once, but she would have none of it, and fighting her would cost more in her energy expended than going over the hills in the first place. Emily had been in and seen more of these races than he ever hoped to. Seeing no one near them as a threat, Omaha relaxed and gave her her head.

Emily's ears flicked back, then forward eagerly, as she took full advantage of the new freedom Omaha was offering her. There was no sluggishness, no strain to her movements. Under Griz's tutelage she was superbly conditioned and still fresh as she attacked one hill after another without the slightest hesitation. Omaha could see thick clouds of dust rising wherever another horse was running. There was no set path within the course where the horses had to run. It was cross-country, and as long as they covered the same distance and ended back at the starting line, the exact course each negotiated would not be questioned. The hills did not allow for much maneuvering among the riders, other than trying to pick the fastest and easiest way through them.

A thick plume of dust was off to Omaha's

left. It could be no other than Jethro, and his horse still had to be running strong for him to be keeping an almost parallel course to Emily as she whipped up one hill and down the next. And he could hear the even drumming of hoofs which told him a couple of horses were not far behind. It was almost impossible for Emily to gain any ground while they were still in the hills, slipping and sliding amongst the loose rocks and gagging dust, but she was holding the narrow lead she had taken when she had slipped free of the box, avoiding catastrophe by mere inches. Omaha saw the end of the hilly stretch coming up ahead, and he lightly pulled Emily in a bit to give her a breather before the hard work ahead. Emily obeyed his request without fighting him, seeming to know that for the moment she was again out front.

Cinnamon ran hard until she reached the camp, its canvas and wood buildings completely deserted, all of its residents strung out along the course of the race to watch. Wildly, she stared around her like a cornered animal looking for a hole to hide in. Then she turned and fled into one of the gambling tents. She paused inside. The only other such establishment she had been in since she hit Kingman's camp had been Mac's place, and there she had been protected by Belle and the formidable power she wielded there. She was not quite sure she should be here in spite of the yawning emptiness that had greeted her bespangled entrance. Still, she almost had herself convinced to stay there and lie low until the race was over and she was sure she could locate Omaha when she heard footsteps. They were even, weighty, and, worse, unhurried, headed with dead certainty straight for her hiding place.

Dashing to the tent flap, Cinnamon moved the canvas just enough to let one eye peek out into the deserted street. Haqihana was heading up the street, his footsteps angling in the direction of the tent she occupied. There was no mistake about it. A grim smile played about his lips, and his angular face looked even harder than Cinnamon remembered it. On tiptoe, Cinnamon dashed for the back of the tent, slid under the canvas, and circled up the street behind the flimsy buildings.

When they came out of the hills, the horses caked with sweat and dust, there were only six riders left. Fully half of the starting field had been lost. To Omaha's displeasure those remaining included both Jethro Clayton and the maniac with the stick. Both of them had managed to stay close during the rough stuff as Emily preferred a flat to really pour on the speed and start to move like a bounding deer. Omaha could feel the

distinct shift in her stride as they came off
the last hill and the flats that ran at the foot
of the mines opened up before her. There
was still a long way to go, and there were no
people along this stretch to urge them on, so
Omaha prepared to pace Emily, saving her
for that final dash through town and again
out into the valley back to the starting line.
For the moment what he was most
concerned with was keeping clear of trouble.

Surprisingly, Emily obediently shortened
her stride when Omaha asked it, taking a
breather almost as if she knew what he was
doing and had the same strategy for the race
in mind. Omaha did not have any doubt
about their ability to win now. All he had to
do was keep his distance from the rider with
the stick, an idea Emily was all for.

What Omaha had not counted on was one
of the riders a little further back. A
square-set man with huge, muscular
shoulders and a bearded face who had
apparently had experience at more than
being a miner, loosened the rope from his
saddle and prepared to use it cowboy style.
Omaha, being in the lead, was his natural
target. The rope whistled in the air above the
man's head as he spun it and urged his horse
to move faster while the others were
slackening off, resting their mounts.

Suddenly, Omaha was aware of the
changing pattern of hoof-beats behind him.

He half turned in his saddle to get a look, but it was already too late. Emily swerved sharply as she caught sight of the rope headed in her direction, fearing it was meant to settle over her neck, but instead of pulling Omaha clear of the rope, it only helped jerk him out of the saddle as the loop settled over his shoulders.

Always one for fast thinking, Omaha rolled as he hit the hard, dusty earth, coming up on one knee to brace himself. The burly man with the cowboy's trick had expected nothing like that and was caught totally unawares. The rope snapped taut between them as his horse plunged on and with a wild yelp he came flying out of the saddle before he could even think to let go of the rope.

Knife flashing almost instantly his goal was accomplished, Omaha cut himself free of the rope, ran the few steps that separated him from the snorting, blowing Emily, and vaulted back into the saddle as she leapt again into a run. The others were ahead of them now, but Omaha had confidence in the little horse. It was just as Griz had said. She had been born to run. This time Omaha urged her forward, talking softly into the ear that continually flicked back toward him while the other remained pricked forward, centered on her goal.

Her gait smooth as an ocean swell, Emily started eating away at the distance they had lost, gaining with astonishing speed. He caught up with stragglers well before they reached the mines, leaving them in his dust, unbelieving expressions on their faces as Emily plowed on for the lead. She reached the rough rider with the stick and her hustling hoofs carried her past him with a rush as her strides seemed to come ever faster. Omaha was sitting quietly in the saddle now, not urging anything more of her, knowing she was already giving it all. Shifting his weight to her advantage, he prepared himself to sit out the ride.

Omaha and Emily caught and passed Jethro on the flats ahead of the mines just before they reached the narrow road that turned back toward camp. With her nose again in the lead scooping in fresh air free of anyone else's dust, Emily slacked off, taking one last breather before the last long run for the finish line. They swept around the bend in the road with a rush of hoofs and the rhythmic clatter of Jethro's horse not too distant behind them. Having learned his lesson, Omaha kept his ears attuned to what was going on in the rear as he swept toward the camp, and suddenly the even pounding that had proclaimed Jethro's nearness was gone. Emily seemed puzzled as well, her ears flicking back and sideways as if she suspected a trick of the kind she was long used to in these races.

As they bore down on the cluster of tents and makeshift buildings that made up Kingman's camp, Omaha glanced over his shoulder. Jethro Clayton was no longer anywhere in evidence, and the other remaining riders were far behind as Emily pulled away from them with every stride. But what happened to Jethro? His horse had not gone down. Omaha had heard nothing, he had just disappeared.

Cinnamon spotted the horses running along the old mine trail as she skirted the camp along the outside, trying to keep buildings of some substance between herself and Haqihana, who gave every appearance each time she caught a glimpse of him, of thoroughly enjoying the entire situation. He was playing a game, and Cinnamon was sure she would not like the ending. She doubted that Haqihana even realized the seriousness in her determination to get away from him, not that he would care if he did.

When Cinnamon looked up again at the running horses, they were moving fast, one far in the lead, the others strung out behind. It was Emily in the lead, Cinnamon had no doubt of that. No other horse ran like her. And, only a few strides behind her, Cinnamon blinked in surprise, was Jethro. She would recognize that flying black coat, black hat, and stiff way he sat the saddle anywhere. The others were much too far behind for any kind of consideration at all. It was Omaha she had her eye on. Then, suddenly, she realized that there was a large open spot behind him. Jethro was nowhere to be seen. Then she saw the thicket of brush and rock below the trail that some maniac might be able to negotiate on horseback if he had enough determination and luck to turn it into a shortcut. At almost the same instant, she again spotted Jethro.

A mass of scratches, bruises, and rips in his clothes, but there Jethro was, bearing down on her on horseback, and Cinnamon knew only too well that he was after her. She darted around the comer, as light on her feet as a fairy, and almost ran headlong into Haqihana as he continued to walk calmly up the street in her direction. Pulling herself up short, Cinnamon froze, the sound of galloping hoofs pounding against her eardrums on one hand, the sight of Haqihana's amused, victorious smile on the other. It was ridiculous. Cinnamon felt like a prize mouse fought over by a pair of cats. Then she saw Omaha.

As far as she was concerned, he looked like a knight in shining armor as he turned down the main street and charged straight in her direction. Unfortunately, Jethro was closer. Jethro was an excellent rider, if a bit crazy, and he was as aware of Omaha's impending presence as Cinnamon. With a wild lunge forward, he headed for Cinnamon, intending to snatch her from the street, on the run, as he had snatched her from the river only days before. Cinnamon sidestepped like a bull fighter. Jethro passed her by, then wheeled to try again. Haqihana was closer. He had no idea of what was going on between the pair, but it was interesting and he had been looking for some amusement to pass the time while he was waiting. If it was a contest over possession of the girl, he was willing to join in.

Haqihana reached for Cinnamon, and she eluded him, ducking behind a post in front of one of the numerous saloons as Jethro made his second pass. Haqihana dashed after Cinnamon as Jethro leaned from the saddle to snag her. Somehow she slipped clear and what Jethro snagged was Haqihana. Haqihana stiffened, his hand shot out in a fist, solidly connecting with Jethro's face, lifting him clear of the saddle. The maneuver was slick, but not slick enough. Jethro chose to fall forward instead of back, and the pair went down in a confused tumble in the middle of the street.

'Omaha!' Cinnamon shrieked as he tore up the street in his haste to reach her, and Haqihana extricated himself from the tangle to make another try.

The strange scene in the street had hit Omaha between the eyes as he had brought

Emily in for the last leg of the race. Instantly, it had been clear to him what was happening. Cinnamon was plainly the object of attention between both Haqihana and Jethro, who had obviously somehow spotted her from the trail and taken a shortcut to intercept her. In that red dress it would have been easy to catch sight of her. In the bright sunlight her sparkles could be seen for miles. But what was going on, though, was a mystery, a mystery only Cinnamon would have the key to unlock.

All Omaha was sure of was he had to do something about it, and he still had a race to win. He tugged on the reins, slowing Emily's pace as he bore down on the strange trio. Emily protested, snorting and tossing her head in anger. The race was not yet over. She was not prepared to stop in her tracks. Omaha started to fight her, demanding more, shortening the reins. Emily buckjumped, swerved, and careened crazily down the street, but her strides shortened and abruptly turned into a jarring trot as she turned in a wheeling dance, fighting the hand that held her back. Omaha was leaning low off the side of his saddle and he managed to half straighten Emily out as they came up alongside Cinnamon, who stood her ground like a proud Joan of Arc. Still vexed, Emily continued on in the same bone-jarring, teeth-rattling trot that did more than telegraph her displeasure at the delay.

Omaha's arm caught Cinnamon beneath her arms, forcing the breath out of her lungs in a loud ooof as Emily broke again into a run. Cinnamon's eyes widened as she looked up into Omaha's face and felt the horse's pace suddenly increase. Groping for a better handhold she somehow locked her slender arms around Omaha's waist while he clung to her in desperation. Cinnamon's feet skimmed above the ground as Emily, unencumbered by the additional weight, took off like a big bird. Omaha could neither pull Cinnamon up into the saddle with him, nor turn loose his grip on her. Swearing bitterly, he hung on. The finish line was no longer far. He knew he would be able to hold her easily until then. In the distance, behind them, Omaha could hear the insistent pounding of running horses. That had to be Jethro, and the others.

Cinnamon's red spangled dress became a blurr against the landscape as Emily regained her stride and whipped behind the camp's edge, swinging again out onto the valley floor, her hoof-beats muffled in the soft thick grass.

The crowd cheered as Omaha approached the finish line. Griz was standing apart from the rest, waving and jumping up and down like a wild man. He knew the race was won. No one was even anywhere close who could challenge Omaha. And, while all those present could not ignore the addition of Cinnamon, her skirts plastered against her in the wind, Omaha was going to cross the finish line first and, in this race, that was all that mattered. Omaha was content to let Emily run for home until he saw something.

Otto appeared at the valley's edge, his horse running hard in their direction. And it did not look like he was just exercising his horse. He was moving fast, and his horse was working hard. Omaha knew it meant trouble, the trouble they had been expecting.

The finish line whipped beneath Emily's flying hoofs as the gathered crowd roared its approval, but as Griz stepped forward to take the reins and give Omaha a congratulatory slap on the back, Omaha turned Emily and kept going. A disbelieving look on his face, Griz stared after them, then he saw Otto, and a grim, set look replaced it. He needed a good horse and he needed it fast.

Omaha was halfway across the valley to intercept Otto when his arm suddenly cramped, reminding him of what he still held in his grip, and whose arms were still tightly wrapped about his waist like a constricting leather thong. He did not want to do it, but from where he sat, he had no choice. He pulled Emily up abruptly and she responded instantly.

'Get down,' Omaha ordered Cinnamon

shortly as Emily came to a standstill.

'What?' Cinnamon demanded, her tone questioning as if she did not understand what she had heard.

'Get off the horse,' Omaha repeated, an edge to his voice, his arm loosing its grip around her at the same time.

Without his strength to hold her, Cinnamon slid down to sit, startled, in the valley's thick green grass.

'Wait a minute,' she shouted, 'you can't...' But her last words were lost to Omaha's ears as he touched his heels to Emily and they were off again to intercept Otto.

A bit off balance in the light of what had just happened, Cinnamon glanced around, but then the sight of Jethro pounding toward her restored her equilibrium in the blink of an eye. In a bound she was on her feet, running back toward the finish line, where the crowd was still gathered, celebrating, unaware of what was happening before their collective noses. She had no chance of reaching them before Jethro caught up with her, but Jethro positively turned her stomach, and Cinnamon was not about to sit there and wait for him to catch up with her again.

'I saw them,' Otto breathlessly imparted the news as he and Omaha came abreast of each other.

His voice was hoarse, and his accent seemed to get thicker when he was agitated as he shifted back and forth from one language to another. Omaha was hard pressed to understand all that Otto was trying to put across, but he got the main body of what he was saying and that was all he needed.

The supply train was coming in from the southeast, and the Indians had already been trailing it when Otto spotted it, though they had not yet taken any action against it. They were waiting then, and Omaha knew there could only be one they were waiting for. Haqihana. When Omaha looked in the direction Otto had been pointing, he saw the thin column of smoke rising from the horizon and drifting skyward. The smoke did not carry any recognizable message, but Omaha knew it could only be a signal for Haqihana to join the tribe where they were setting their trap for the pack train. Omaha's suspicions were confirmed when Haqihana separated himself from the crowd, on horseback now, and headed at a run for the distant spire of smoke, a white thread against a blue sky.

Wheeling Emily fast, Omaha started her back for the camp with Otto hot on his heels. They would have to move fast if they were going to use the plan, such as it was, that he had devised. And he knew they would have to use it. It was the only one they had. There was only one problem as Omaha saw it, and it was heading for Cinnamon. Jethro Clayton. Cinnamon was running at an angle away from him, but there was no question that he would catch her. Omaha swore. He needed her to help him with his wings.

Emily, seemingly tireless under Omaha's hand, galloped up to Cinnamon. 'Get on!' Omaha shouted at her above the rising wind and the rising thud of hoofbeats at Jethro's approach.

'What?' Cinnamon shrieked as she whirled in mid-stride, startled at Omaha's sudden reappearance.

'Get on the horse!' he repeated, reaching a hand down to her as he kicked his left foot free of the stirrup.

Thoroughly confused, but not about to question the command, Cinnamon placed her hand in his and swung up behind him light as a feather. They broke into a full gallop and Cinnamon buried her face in Omaha's shoulder as they charged at Jethro head on, none of them breaking stride. At the last instant, Emily swerved almost simultaneously with Jethro's horse and they continued on in opposite directions for many strides before Jethro managed to get his horse turned again and headed after them. Omaha knew he had to get Jethro off his tail before he could launch himself with any hope of success, but he was not sure how to do it with so little time. Otto's horse ran easily at their side, but Otto was not a brawler, and Jethro was not his problem, those mule skinners with the pack train were.

Then Omaha spotted Griz glancing around feverishly like he was looking for something to do, and Omaha decided to give it to him. He shifted Emily's strides a bit, swinging her back toward the finish line of the race they had won. Almost instantly Griz spotted them, and no words were needed between them to get the message across. He stood there, a broad, beefy bear of a man, and Omaha could have sworn he saw a glitter in those hawklike green eyes when they whipped past him.

As they passed, Omaha looked over his shoulder to see Griz take a casual half pace forward, reach up when Jethro came alongside, and just as casually jerk him clear of the saddle. Jethro gave a startled yelp as his horse came to an abrupt standstill and Griz himself piled into the leather, and took off in the wake of Omaha's passage.

CHAPTER FIFTEEN

Omaha swept up the deserted street, retrieving Griz's mule, the wings still strapped to her pack saddle, and headed without pause for the highest building in the camp with Griz and Otto hot on his heels. An elaborate four-story structure, the highest building in Kingman's camp was made of heavy timbers such as the men used to shore up the insides of the mines, with canvas covering the wooden skeleton to form the walls. It housed a saloon on the ground floor, a gambling casino on the second, and the top two floors were given over to the ladies who had the boomingest business in the camp.

When they pulled up in front of the imposing four-story structure, Emily was blowing, her head dropping some. Finally, she had run her limit. Omaha piled out of the saddle, dragging Cinnamon with him, and fell to untying the wings as she wordlessly joined him on the opposite side, pulling at the ropes that held the wooden framework.

'What exactly you aimin' to do, boy?' Griz queried as Omaha unbuckled his gun belt, hastily rearranging it so he could buckle it across his chest, leaving the holster with its gun within easy reach once he was airborne.

Not for a minute did Omaha believe he would do anything other than catch a convenient air current and glide off to the battlefield. After all, both times in the past he had launched himself from high places he had met with success. His average was far too high to expect any other result.

'I'm not exactly sure,' Omaha admitted. He glanced at Otto. 'I know what the chief and his people want, the whiskey and supplies, but what the hell is there about a supply train that a man like Haqihana would want?' Omaha demanded an answer, realizing now, suddenly, that Otto had been with them. Otto could supply the answer he sought.

Looking a little hesitant, Otto was not sure he should be giving away secrets, even now. As if to make sure there were no other ears listening in, he glanced hastily around. 'Money.' He uttered the word quickly as if it burned his tongue. 'Pay for many miners who are working for the big mines in camp,' Otto said quickly, his accent thicker than ever in his agitation. 'Before, when they try to send it in a strongbox by stage, they often get robbed. Once, they even send it with cavalry. So they think to try it this way. But,' Otto added hastily, 'how could anyone know? We did not know until far out on trail, far from any town. No one on the train could have told.'

'Haqihana knows,' Omaha said grimly as the wings came free from their moorings and he almost swung Cinnamon around the back of the mule in his haste to get inside and upstairs.

The facts hit home. There could be no

other explanation. Otto realized it as he spilled out of the saddle to follow Omaha and Cinnamon. Behind him, Griz still sat his horse, now gazing off in the direction Haqihana had taken only minutes before. Omaha had all the help he could use right here, and Griz had a score to settle where Haqihana was concerned, a debt to be paid. That breed had been riding roughshod over those parts long enough. He had killed his coyote, Ezra, and now it was likely that he would kill crazy Omaha if he succeeded in flying into his guns. That was something Griz did not want to risk. He knew he could not take on Haqihana face to face, but there had been nothing put down in writing about a man being sneaky, and that was where Griz excelled. With one last glance at the doorway where Omaha, Cinnamon, and Otto had disappeared, Griz wheeled his borrowed horse around and lit out cross-country.

Between Omaha and Cinnamon, hauling the wings sideways, they got the wings to the top of the building. The canvas walls billowed and swayed as they scaled the stairs at a rate that left Cinnamon gasping for breath when they reached the end of their climb. Otto, panting, topped the stairs right behind them. Omaha stared up at the peaked, canvased roof from the inside when they reached the top floor. There was only one thing he could do, and he pulled out his knife to do it.

Monkeylike, Omaha crawled up a couple of the skeletal crossbeams, and, with an overhead swing, swept his glittering knife blade through the canvas. A loud ripping snap sounded as Omaha continued to drag the knife through the canvas time and again with brutal swiftness. As the canvas fell away a large hole began to open up in the roof, and Omaha kept working. It seemed like it took a long time, but only short minutes had passed before Omaha had a huge hole cut in the canvas, a hole large enough to allow his unwieldy wings to pass through to the outside.

Crawling through first, Omaha reached down to catch one tip of the wings and start hauling them up after him as Otto stood on the floor pushing from the bottom, and Cinnamon stood on top of one of the girls' dressers, guiding them from the side. Outside, Cinnamon could hear the wind whistling around the top of the building, and the flap of the canvas where it slapped sharply against itself, the shreds where Omaha had cut it flying before the wind.

For a moment, as Omaha crawled up and out on the main crossbeam that ran across the length of the building at its peak, Cinnamon feared he would be swept to the ground by the rising wind catching his wings before he was ready. But he managed to keep a low profile until first Cinnamon, then Otto, joined him. Then, standing sideways to the wind so his wings cut it instead of captured it for flight, Omaha waited impatiently as Otto and Cinnamon teetered on either side of him, tying the leather thongs that held the wings in place.

'Where's Griz?' Omaha asked as he peered down through the gaping hole he had cut. But, even as he asked the question, he knew. He muttered under his breath as the wind tugged and plucked at his clothes like persistent, if gentle, fingers.

To Cinnamon's dreamy-eyed stare, Omaha looked like a wild, heroic adventurer standing there, braced against the wind, his thick, glossy black hair rippling like a field of spring grass. Again she yearned to fly with him, but knew this was not the time. With hasty jerks she finished tying the thongs, staring up into his face, his cheeks whipped to a ruddy hue, as she did. In just a very short time he could be killed. The thought swept through Cinnamon's mind and for a moment she clutched his outstretched arm, her blue eyes eloquently expressing her concern. Then, just as abruptly, she swept the thought aside, crawling down to a lower beam so Omaha could launch himself without sweeping her from the roof to the hard ground quite a distance below them.

Otto did the same, retreating when his job

was complete, clutching at the rough wood for support as he hung over it like a sack of wheat. He had come up in such haste to assist that he had completely forgotten how many years had passed since he had done such a thing, and his sense of balance had never been acute. He wondered how he was going to get safely down, but now was not the time to bring up such a thing to his companions. In a moment more, Omaha would be gone, sailing on the wind, and he would have only Cinnamon, clinging precariously to her own beam to assist him.

Stepping to the edge of the peak, Omaha swung his wings full into the wind. For a moment he stood there, leaning into the wind, legs locked inside buckskin leggings against the force of it. Then Cinnamon saw a faint smile appear at the corners of his lips, and he stepped off into space.

For a breathless moment the wind billowed beneath the wings, swinging him high into a sky so blue it almost hurt Cinnamon's eyes to follow his flight. Almost directly above them he was spiraling upward like a leaf caught on the wind, then suddenly there was a pause. He hovered like a butterfly with fragile wings outstretched, then, just as suddenly, he was gliding, being swept along at astonishing speed and in the right direction. Cinnamon gasped, putting one hand over her mouth as Omaha zoomed toward the valley with all the speed of a hunting falcon.

From her perch high atop the canvas saloon, casino, and brothel, Cinnamon could see tiny figures still moving around in the valley beyond. She could see the shadowy, silhouetted heads turning skyward as if directed by some invisible hand pulling strings on so many puppets. Then, to the last man, they turned almost in unison and started after Omaha as he courted and rode the winds far above them. Cinnamon groaned, then noticed something else even more worthy of her distress. She hoped it was just her imagination, but something deep inside told her it was not. Omaha's glide path was set in a distinctly downward direction. Would he even make it as far as the pack train before the ground swept up to meet him, leaving him alone, on foot, and in a distinctly unpleasant situation? She knew then she had to be near him, just in case.

Forgetting all about Otto being on top of the timbers with her, she swung a leg over, revealing a patch of white thigh, and slid through the opening to the dresser top below. Only one thing was in her mind, and that was to get moving fast.

'Wait!' Otto exploded as Cinnamon suddenly disappeared from view. 'Wait,' he called again, not certain she had heard him the first time.

Below, Cinnamon froze, undecided what to do. She heard Otto calling her, but she wanted to go after Omaha, had to go after Omaha. Still, she could not leave Otto in such a predicament. Cinnamon wanted to scream in frustration. She had to go, but she could not. Rooted to the spot, she was torn between one and the other.

Shifting his weight, Otto tried to make his way back to the opening Omaha had made in the canvas, fearing Cinnamon had not heard his cries and had already gone. A few moments of silence passed, then Otto heard the first, almost indiscernible, sounds of cloth tearing. Something gave beneath him and Otto grabbed for the timber that lay across the peak from which Omaha had launched himself.

It was happening all too fast. Cinnamon too heard the now unmistakable rippling of canvas above her. She gave a little squeak of apprehension and then Otto's legs and lower body came through the canvas with a loud splitting of canvas and a bellowed foreign oath Cinnamon could not begin to understand. She flew to the dresser, climbing back on it with no notice as to how she accomplished the feat so quickly and grabbed hold of Otto's dangling legs as if she could somehow keep him from falling that way. Otto felt the sudden pressure on his legs, and on his arms and shoulders where they still gripped determinedly the rough timber.

'Nein, Liebschen, nein!' Otto called out to her, but his voice was muffled by the canvas that surrounded his middle like a billowing sack.

If she would let go he knew he could drop safely to the floor below. But, if he dropped with her attached to him as she was, he would pull her down as well. Otto tried to call out to her again, but it was already too late. His grip on the heavy timber weakening, he could not hold on any longer. With a strangled cry, Otto's grip was torn loose by the weight of his body and he felt himself falling. The floor was not far below his feet, but he landed with a heavy thud, Cinnamon coming down on top of him from her perch atop the dresser.

For a moment Otto had the breath knocked out of him, but it did not last long, and neither he nor Cinnamon paused to consider any further damage. They were of one mind and almost collided getting through the door and heading back down the stairs. There was no time to lose.

As Omaha drifted on the wind, the old feeling of exhilaration rushed through him in a wave. Air blew cold against his face, and Omaha, as usual, fought to discover the secrets of controlled flight. But, for the moment, there was not much he dared try.

Already heading in the right direction, a mistake could send him careening off into the surrounding hills with no hope of getting back in time.

On outstretched wings he swept past the valley with tremendous speed he could remember only duplicating when he had crossed the river in his downward glide. He was aware of the downward tendencies of this flight, but he was even more aware of the people far below. He had caught their eyes to a man, and all were gazing up in his direction, heads thrown back, in silent observance of his passage. Then, suddenly, Omaha saw the crowd starting to move. It swayed as if it were one continuous mass, each within it attached to another, then the crowd was moving rapidly along in his wake. He wanted to yell to them to go back, but Omaha doubted that they would either hear, or listen. He could only hope the rising wind would soon carry him well beyond them and they would give up their raucous pursuit.

Far ahead, Griz was nothing more than a speck on the landscape to Omaha's gaze, but growing larger as each passing second swept Omaha along toward his goal. Haqihana was nowhere in sight, but the hills were plentiful, and he could easily be behind one, riding out of sight. Squinting his eyes against the force of the wind, Omaha searched in the distance for his first glimpse of the supply train, and its proximity to the Indians who were planning the raid. He had only a few short minutes to decide what to do after he located them. His gun was located now within easy reach, as was his knife, but Omaha had come out here to avert a massacre, not partake in one. He still did not know how he was going to do it.

All at once, an idea flashed through his mind. Glancing down again he saw the people of Kingman's camp, losing ground behind him, but plugging determinedly on. They would not arrive at the scene of the attack with him, but they would be close behind, within sight, when he swooped in on the scene. If he could manage to land near there, it was possible he could talk to the old chief. After all, Omaha was half Sioux. If he could convince the Indians that the men of the mining camp knew what was going to happen, and were coming en masse to stop it, it was possible he could convince them to give it up. Get them to ride back into the hills before there was real trouble. The only problem then would be Haqihana. By the very nature Haqihana had displayed in the saloon, he would not be willing to give up easily. And, if what Otto had told them was true, the problem would be increased tenfold. The key to his success would lie in his ability to convince the old chief to abandon Haqihana and his ill-conceived plans.

Behind him, Omaha could hear shouts and yells of the exuberant crowd from Kingman's camp as they trailed him. Ahead, just within view, was the supply train winding its way, like a sluggish worm, up the broad pass that led through the hills toward the camp that lay to the northeast. And, on the hills beyond, perched in readiness, were the Indians. Omaha thought that if he had seen them, then perhaps the trail-hardened mule skinners with the supply train had also seen them and would be ready and waiting. With the element of surprise gone, Omaha shuddered to think of the results.

Though aware of the continuing drop in his altitude as the wind bore him along Omaha was not worried as he was headed directly for a spot that lay between the moving supply train, the waiting Sioux, and the approaching crowd from Kingman's camp. He planned on coming down. There was no way he could be of help to the situation while still on the wing. His good fortune was almost unbelievable. He was dropping at a rate that would put him down almost exactly where he desired to be. Omaha knew well the superstitions and religion of the Sioux people. Alighting before them from out of the sky would be impressive. It would certainly help get his point across. Again Omaha glanced backward at the trailing crowd from the camp, then at the supply train now bristling with rifles held in the hands of the men and propped beside the legs of the drivers, and back to the Indians waiting patiently atop a hill. He was dropping lower rapidly. It was as if the Fates were riding with him at last.

Then Omaha spotted Haqihana approaching the waiting Indians from an angle that took him well out of the sight of the slow-moving pack train. From his bird's-eye view, Omaha also spotted Griz's determined approach. Omaha did not see how Haqihana could be aware of him yet, but Omaha was more than aware of the two specks moving across the open valley from the camp, heading rapidly in his direction. He did not want to think about who it might be, he already knew. Cinnamon and Otto.

For a moment Omaha was distracted. When he again took in the entire situation, the Indians were already spilling down the side of the hill heading for the supply train, and Haqihana was moving to intercept and join them. Omaha grimaced. It was happening too fast. They had not even taken notice of his presence. Abruptly, Omaha remembered the gun now hanging from his chest. He might yet do some good if he could draw their attention, pull them up short.

Eagerly, Omaha reached for the thongs that Cinnamon had tied to free one arm and

235

enable him to draw the gun. Omaha had not had reason until that moment to try the bindings, and it was then he found out they had been knotted by Cinnamon's nervous fingers and could not be untied.

Omaha groaned, swinging his weight with a sharp snap from side to side as he snatched at the leather bindings, trying to jerk them loose in spite of his own growing awareness that he was not going to be able to do it. Strapped to his wings, helpless, and continuing to lose altitude, there was little doubt in his mind that he was going to drop right into the middle of a blazing battle and not be able to do a thing to protect himself, let alone help anyone else.

Jerking more determinedly at the thongs as he drifted lower over the converging opponents, suddenly, he felt his course shift. Instantly, Omaha let go of the thongs and tried madly to right himself as he swayed quickly into a careening pinwheel across the bright afternoon sky, his oversized shadow springing into sharp relief on the ground below.

Heads jerked up toward Omaha, both human and animal, regarding him with equal surprise as he swept low above them in a tight circle that almost amounted to spinning on one wing tip in midair. For a moment it was as if time stood still. Though the Indians still plunged forward, the wild cries and war whoops died in their throats. As the supply train lumbered to a complete halt, jovial shouts of approaching camp citizens could be heard, carrying on the wind. Omaha fought for control, but had no idea how to regain it, if indeed he had ever had it.

The world spun crazily around Omaha, his giant birdlike shadow swooping and diving along the ground like some gigantic winged hunter in search of prey. His position precarious at best, Omaha had not seen the exact moment the horses began to panic at the sight of his passage. Skimming over the tops of the wagons, he tucked his legs up to keep from colliding with the canvas, and became suddenly aware of the panic that had started off with one lone horse and was spreading rapidly from one animal to the next throughout the pack train and the Indian ponies. With all the control over his flight that an autumn leaf had when it was jerked free from a tree, Omaha rode the swiftly changing air currents. One moment he would be spiraling skyward, the clear blueness of it dazzling to his eyes, the next he would be plummeting toward the earth with appalling speed, and below, bedlam had spread totally through both sides, the Indians as well as the mule skinners.

Indian ponies were bucking furiously, throwing their riders while mules broke their traces and pack ponies went berserk beneath loads they had packed in safety all the way from St Louis. Omaha's weaving, diving course crisscrossed back and forth across the open pass, giving them no opportunity to settle down before he was whipping overhead again. Guns were out, both sides bristling with them, but neither could use them.

A supply wagon went over sideways as Omaha passed, dangerously low. On impulse Omaha put his feet out as he swung into the thick of the crazed Indian ponies, connecting with one of the braves with a solid whump, taking him neatly off the struggling pony's back. An occasional gun went off, but the bullets went wild, and the sounds Omaha heard most were the terrified and angry whinnies, snorts, shrieks of the panicked animals mingled with the brutal swearing of the mule skinners and guttural Sioux shouting with commanding authority.

Never had Omaha expected anything like this. Emily had not been upset by the sight of him attached to his wings, but then, Emily never panicked over anything that he had ever seen. Both the Indians and the pack train were in total chaos. Neither had the time nor the inclination to attack the other. Men were on foot, having been thrown, and some were on wagons, still struggling with frightened animals that seemed to panic afresh each time Omaha passed over. A few men were astride ponies that bucked, ran, swerved, and reared in an attempt to bolt.

Omaha cringed as he rode the crosscurrents of the mountain pass, knowing each dive could be his last. A wagon started to roll as the mule broke into a lumbering gallop and Omaha saw an Indian pony, bucking for all it was worth, collide with the side of the wagon, leaving his rider clinging with wild desperation to the side of the canvas-topped wagon, his bronzed body outlined starkly against the dingy canvas. And, by craning his neck around to glance over his shoulder, Omaha saw the arrival of the crowd from Kingman's camp. Like a horde of swarming locusts, they spilled over the low rise and into the cut with hardly a pause to take in the situation. What he did not see was Cinnamon. Mounted on Emily, she skirted the edge of the teeming mass sliding back and forth with Omaha's erratic course in an attempt to be near when he came down. Otto had disappeared into the fray, his own horse as unperturbed as Emily at the sight of Omaha soaring overhead.

The pass was littered with men sprawled on the ground, knocked breathless by a rampaging horse or overturned wagon. Others were staggering around, dazed, trying to locate a horse that had galloped off to a safer distance, or just wandering amongst the fallen men and debris in disbelief.

239

The people from Kingman's camp poured onto the bizarre battleground littered not with dead bodies, but with live ones looking for a way out. There seemed to be no threat from either the confused Indian braves or the rattled mule skinners, so the men and women from the race crowd fell to picking up the long before paid-for goods. Supplies they would have to do without for nearly a year if they did not get them now. With jocular good humor held over from the day's entertaining race, they elbowed aside both Indians and mule skinners in their haste to retrieve the scattered supplies.

The earth was strewn with kegs of whiskey lying on their sides, bolts of cloth opened and blowing in the breeze, sacks of coffee, sugar, flour, and salt in heaps like downed soldiers. A broken sack of spangles for dance hall dresses spewed its contents in a shifting, glittering pattern over the grass. Pots and pans, needles and pins, boots and shoes lay scattered beside or behind broken or overturned wagons and split packs. Spools of thread spun a gossamer web upon the tips of the soft grass where the end had come loose and the spool unwound.

Omaha felt a difference in the wind, another drop in his altitude, and this time he knew from past experience that he was coming down. A pair of Indian braves with a skittish, but quieted horse scooped up a couple of sacks of flour and coffee and lit out for the hills. Others followed rapidly and for a moment, Omaha breathed a sigh of relief.

Then he heard the gunshot. With amazement, Omaha eyed the small round hole that opened up in the leather of his wings near his left shoulder, and gave a start as a second shot opened another hole above his head. A third shot cracked almost beside him, jerking his attention directly before him as the bullet whipped beneath his arm. Dropping like a stone, Omaha now was in a steep glide. He saw Haqihana lift his gun to fire at him again, Griz pounding down on his heels unbeknownst to him, an instant before Omaha plummeted right into him.

Their bodies impacted with an audible thud as Haqihana's horse began to rear. The gun Haqihana had been clenching flew off into the deep grass and they hung there an instant, suspended by circumstance, before the wind flipped Omaha's wings, sending them both crashing to the ground with a splintering, crackling sound as they hit the earth. Again, in an attempt to free himself, Omaha began pulling madly at the knotted thongs. Haqihana rose above him in a cold murderous rage. The gold, now, was out of his reach, but Omaha was not.

His black eyes chilled to their depth, his angular face twisted with the rage of Satan denied, Haqihana fell on him, his long fingers locking about Omaha's throat where he lay flat on his back like a flipped turtle, unable to raise even a hand in his own defense. Omaha's eyes bulged as he felt the unrelenting pressure, the intensifying grip on his throat. Black wings fluttered before his eyes as he brought his knees up, and with a desperate lunge, broke Haqihana's grip, throwing him to sprawl backwards in the grass. With superhuman effort, Omaha lunged to his feet, coming off his back like an acrobat, his wings damaged, but still very firmly attached.

Haqihana was down only an instant before he came for Omaha again, murder in his eyes. With an instinct for survival, Omaha swung the wings sharply. The broken tip caught Haqihana across the head and shoulder, sending him to the earth a second time. Regaining his feet, Haqihana went after Omaha again, a bit more wary, but just as intent.

A breeze blew. Omaha, his wings outstretched, staggered backwards before it. Haqihana followed, oblivious to Griz's imminent arrival. The wind continued to blow, and Omaha continued to stagger before it until he managed to dig his heels in and flip the edge of his wings to the wind. Haqihana grinned tightly and lunged for him. Omaha tried a repeat of his wing trick, attempting to catch Haqihana with the edge

242

and send him sprawling, but he missed. Haqihana drove past him, the momentum of his charge unstoppable. A gust of wind sent Omaha reeling backwards after him, colliding with him, stumbling and landing on top of him, pinning the feared gunman beneath him. There they stayed, Haqihana struggling helplessly beneath Omaha, who remained, the awkward wings still attached, right where he was until Griz dismounted only a few strides away and walked, almost casually, to where the pair lay.

Griz looked at the pair tangled on the ground, Omaha on top of a struggling Haqihana, then glanced at the battleground where no blood had been spilled. In disbelief he slowly shook his head. And there was a glint of devilment in his sharp green eyes as Cinnamon pulled Emily to a lock-legged stop almost in front of them, piled out of the saddle, her red dress blazing in the bright sunlight, and threw herself on top of Omaha heedless of Haqihana pinned beneath him. Caught between a struggling, swearing gunman below, and an almost suffocating Cinnamon above, Omaha groaned, looking to Griz in a silent appeal to cut him loose.

Griz, though, was still gazing out across the pass, marveling at the sight he saw there. The Indians, to a man, were gone, taking only a few supplies that could easily be spared, along with them. The debris, broken wagons, supplies, and rampaging mules were spread from one end of the pass to the other, but no one had been killed. And they had Haqihana exactly where they wanted him, though it was a foregone conclusion that no one would know what to do with him.

'Well,' Griz mouthed the words like he was tasting them, 'I'll be damned.'

CHAPTER SIXTEEN

After that eventful Sunday afternoon, Omaha, Griz, Cinnamon, and Otto had not stayed long in Kingman's camp. As Griz had put it, there were things to be done, and races to be won. And Griz had been wrong in assuming there would be none who would know what to do with the half-breed Haqihana. Once the story had been told, the miners had taken him in hand to be held until the next time the U.S. marshal came through. Everyone seemed pretty vague on when that was likely to happen.

Otto had bid them all a fond farewell and had re-established himself with the mule skinners, who were starting back to pick up a new train almost immediately. Before parting company, he had once again taken the time to repair the new holes in Omaha's wings.

Cinnamon had stuck with Omaha and Griz as they had wandered from one town to another and one race to another with Omaha always riding Emily to victory. No one was exactly sure what had become of Jethro, and, not remarkably, no one really cared, except for the vague possibility that lurked in the backs of their minds of his showing up again.

But months had passed, and the months had turned into a year, and no one gave much thought at all to Jethro and Haqihana any more. For the moment there was only one thing that absorbed all their attention. Flying.

El Capitan loomed from the valley floor, stark against the bright orange blaze that colored the sky with sunrise. Far below, Cinnamon's horse, Emily, and Griz's mule had been picketed where there had been at least some dry scrub for them to nibble on, and they were alone.

High on the precipice above, Omaha Jones stood firm, arms outstretched beneath his wings, the sunrise at his back. He had returned to his beginning, his roots. Here was where he had started, and here was where he must begin again. This time he faced the west instead of the east and the wind blew sweetly against his face, almost beckoning to him. He felt the coolness of it wash over him, felt the bite of it as lungs expanded, drinking in the air as if it were clear spring water. The tug of the wind was against his wings and he heard Griz's querulous mutterings behind him. Cinnamon was there too, standing silently to one side after she had assisted him in donning his wings, her knuckles pressed against her white teeth. It was to be a simple glide to the earth much like the one he had while crossing the river, and again from the tall building at Kingman's camp. He remembered well the last flight he had taken from atop El Capitan, but that had been a fluke. Nothing like it could ever happen again. Flying, it was plain, was good only for short distances. Some much shorter than others.

This time Omaha had checked and rechecked to make sure Cinnamon had tied the thongs properly so he could release them when he reached the ground. All the day before the three of them had spent in the arduous climb, fighting the stubborn mountain. Then there had been the night of rest and preparation and now finally, Omaha Jones was ready. The red of sunrise spread rapidly across the valley, sending long shadows before it and the brightening of the blue sky sent a warmth shooting through the chilled morning air.

Omaha breathed the air, the mingling of warmth and chill, in long deep breaths as he opened his eyes to the blueness of the

246

heavens above and the dun-colored sand of the valley below. For a moment longer he stood there, casting a last tender look in Cinnamon's direction, then leaned forward into the blowing wind and left solid ground behind.

Omaha dipped like a swooping falcon and Cinnamon gasped as she rushed to the edge where he had stepped clear. Below, she saw him level off and start to rise again on the air currents, floating like a feather on the wind. Blue eyes wide with apprehension, Cinnamon let her caught-up breath out in a long sigh, but she knew it was not over yet. He rose again, even higher until he was flying almost level with the top of the plateau from where he had launched himself, but he was not circling, or dropping toward the ground as expected. Instead, he was headed nearly due west, and showed no signs of dropping lower, or altering course.

The old exhilaration Omaha had felt on his first flight was there. Soaring, conquering the wind, he reveled in the old feeling of power, and it was some time before he realized that his altitude was not diminishing. To the contrary, he seemed as high, or possibly higher than when he had started. Craning his neck, Omaha could see back over his shoulder, and what he saw gave him a start. There, far in the distance, rose the hulk of El Capitan, and atop it, hardly visible any longer, were two tiny specks that had to be Griz and Cinnamon.

Alarmed, Omaha threw his weight from side to side in an attempt to pull himself down. He swore in English and hurled foul epithets in Sioux as a fresh gust of air caught him anew, hurrying him along, giving him no choice in the matter. Quickly, the terrain below was changing. It was happening again. As the wind swept him along, Omaha gritted his teeth and waited. He would have to come down somewhere. But his thoughts kept turning to Cinnamon. What was she going to think when he disappeared like a speck of dust in the far distance? Somehow, he knew, he was going to have to find Cinnamon again.

Griz swore in unison with Omaha though neither of them knew it. Staring after Omaha he gave Cinnamon a sage look as if observing a very disobedient child.

'He's gone and done it again,' he mused, no longer in the least bit surprised by Omaha's turnabouts.

Cinnamon nodded dumbly, gazing after the rapidly diminishing speck against the blueness of the morning sky. 'What's out that way?' she asked numbly.

'Wal,' Griz ruminated on that for a moment, frowning, then turned to her with a shrug. 'If he goes far enough, there's a ocean out there somewheres.'

Cinnamon's eyes opened even wider. 'An ocean!' Without another word Cinnamon attacked the trail leading down.

The downhill trail was much easier than the uphill climb, and it was not necessary to be careful of the wings as they descended, seeing that Omaha was in total possession of them. In record time Cinnamon and Griz reached the bottom, Cinnamon piling into Emily's saddle without pause. And Griz, after throwing the pack from the mule's back for additional speed and uttering a few choice swearwords in Omaha's direction, climbed up on Cinnamon's horse.

Together they lit out across the dusty valley floor, heading almost due west as the crow flies, a heavy cloud of dust rising from beneath the hoofs of the animals.

P. A. Bechko

was born Peggy Ann Bechko in South Haven, Michigan. She had always loved the American West and visited it frequently. She wrote her first Western, *The Night of the Flaming Guns*, at the age of twenty-two. Her editor at Doubleday was surprised when he saw her full legal name. However, he went on to buy four more Western novels from her. In 1981 Bechko moved to Santa Fe, New Mexico, and with the help of her family, built the house where she now lives. Her latest novel is titled *The Winds of Fortune* and is set in the Pony Express era of 1861. C. L. Sonnichsen writing in EL PASO TIMES described Bechko as 'one of the few women in the business but she outdoes many of her male counterparts in fertility of imagination.'

OL .9122